Da Streets are Callin' Me

By: Mi'shele

Copyright © 2016 by KMG Publications LLC

This is a work of fiction. Names, characters, businesses, places, events and incidents are used in a fictitious manner. Any resemblance to actual persons, living or dead, or actual events is purely coincidental. Actions or situations portrayed in this novel are either products of the author's imaginations or are used fictitiously.

Da Streets are Callin' Me. Copyright © 2016 by KMG Publications. All rights reserved. All novels are manufactured in the United States of America. For information, address KMG Publications, P.O. Box 53513, Indianapolis, IN, 46253.

Library of Congress Cataloging-in-Publication Data

Cover Illustration and design was created by KMG Publications LLC Freelance Designer Copyright © 2016

KMG Publications, LLC
P.O. Box 53513
Indianapolis, IN 46253
Facebook.com/kmgpublicationsllc

> # Discount Code: <u>Pied-Pipers</u>
> *See details below for more information*

This Book is dedicated to all the ones that I have loss:

Narvelle D. Morris

Michael "Turtle Head" Rogers

Christopher Hall

Ronald "Ronnie" Mann II

> *The above-mentioned **"discount code"** is to only be used in conjunction with individuals, detainees, inmates or prisoners house within Correctional Facilities and Lawful Detention establishments. To redeem above-mentioned **"discount code"** individuals, detainees, inmates or prisoners must provide the following: Facility address, Gallery or DOC number and housing location.

Chapter 1-1

It was 10: 40pm. Marion and Liyah were sitting in his black Porsche Cayenne. Liyah was exhausted from being tied up in court for 10+ hours. She was ready to get home and get out of her pant suit and relax. Literally, she gave her closing argument twenty minutes ago before the judge deemed court adjourned for the day. Her mind focused on the prosecutors closing statement set for tomorrow.

They sat in front of Cleveland's local rib spot B-n-M's waiting for their food. Every time they came here, her emotions fluttered. This was where she and Marion first met. She relished the warm summer breeze recalling that day clearly.

> "Her and her older cousin Mya had just left the Arcadia after hours lounge. They chose to get a bite to eat. B-n-M's was the only restaurant willing to stay open after midnight. They were packed that night.
>
> There was vehicles as far as the eye could see; however, a champagne colored Range Rover caught her attention. Two handsome men stepped from the suv and went into B-n-M's. They were well-dressed and groomed.
>
> One was about 6'2', 200pds caramel brown skin with a muscular athletic physique. His button down polo with stone washed jeans where well fitted. He was with a taller light skinned guy with a bald fade; which he called Dave. Mya thought he was so debonair in his silk shirt and slacks.

There were about 30 plus people in the restaurant. Somewhere placing orders while others was hanging out. The two guys from the Range Rover where behind Liyah and Mya in line. Suddenly, a fight broke out. Some lady got bumped into Mya then some man in a red shirt pushed Liyah. They began cussing his ass out when he shoved Liyah into a table.

Before she got up, the guy in the red shirt body slammed some guy in a white beater on his neck. They watched the guy in the beater coward on the ground in pain. He grimaced in agony clutching his drooping right shoulder and collar bone. The 6'2', caramel brown guy confronted the man in the red shirt and said, "try that shit with me!"

The guy was petrified as he started apologizing. He now lacked the aggression he just displayed. People where now throwing food, yelling and cussing as they watched the standoff. The guy he called Dave had the crowd under control as he yelled "Shut the fuck up!"

A lot of the young thugs wanted to see a fight; they kept yelling from the back of the massive crowd "Fuck that nigga, swing on him!" What happened next shocked her. The 6'2', caramel brown guy told the man in the red beater to break his pinky. The caramel guy quickly pulled a gun from his waist and pointed it in the man's face.

After about 3minutes of pleading, the man broke his left pinky. He bent it outwards until it dislocated at the knuckle. "Ah shit," the man yelled in pain. The guy tucked his gun back in his waist.

People began to scatter out of B-n-M's cuz someone yelled "They called the law!" Cars, trucks and motorcycles racing from B-n-M's parking lot. Everyone in town knew about the corrupted ass Cleveland Police Department. They were known for falsely arresting people.

The Range Rover was backing out when Liyah rushed over to their suv. The caramel guy rolled down his window and grinned. Liyah handed him a piece of paper and uttered "call me." He replied "ok. My name is Marion. I'll call you later." Liyah ran to Mya's grey Infiniti and shot out of parking lot. Police sirens whirred from every direction.

After that thought, Liyah texted Mya. She simply said "call me." Marion listened to the radio while waiting on their order. He leaned over and kissed her. Marion's phone rang. Immediately, he stepped out of his truck talking in an East Cleveland lingo.

Behind the truck's tinted windows, Liyah watched a couple argue in front of the B-n-M's. Marion motioned he's about to go get the food as he tapped the window. Liyah called Mya but she did not answer. Simultaneously, she received a text from Deep Stroke. When she looked at the message, it was a video of him jacking off. Suddenly, the sight of his 11 ½ inches of pure back breaking, leg folding chocolate dick got her aroused.

She thought to herself *"God damn!"* She watched the video and her nipples hardened. His moans excited her. She reminisced of when they were last together. She caressed her now moistened panties with the phone in her lap.

"Damn! Why is he fucking teasing me? He trying to be funny," she thought as she closed her eyes.

"Shit I can't be mad. This probably was payback from last week. I told him I could make my pussy squirt," she uttered as she continued watching the video.

She could tell Deep Stroke was about to cum. He moaned loudly and slowly gripped the head of his massive dick tightly. Unexpectedly, Marion tapped the dark tinted passenger window holding up the food. She could only see the words "Thank You" on the side of the bag. Marion lifted the door handle but her door was locked.

She hit the unlock button and pointed to the rear passenger door just as Deep Stroke came. She looked back at the video momentarily. There was an immense amount of cum on his stomach as he started licking it off with his finger. *Lord I love this chocolate freaky motherfucker*" she mumbled.

Marion opened the door so swiftly it caused Liyah to drop her phone. He quickly placed the food on the floor and slammed the door. She fumbled on the floor looking for her phone. She stopped the video just as he opened the driver's door. Liyah could hear Marion talking on the phone as he got in the truck.

"That nigga Quintana tripping! Jay, do you really think Dave is going to sell him two Scottie Pippen's for a tote and a half? Now you and I know D is not going for that at all. Quintana must be snorting that shit he selling! Tell him we need full fare my nigga. But hey, I should be heading your way within the next hour and a half," he said as the other line beeped.

He saw it was Dave and he decided to take the call. He just told Jay he will see him later.

"What up nigga," Marion said as he looked out his tinted window.

"Not a damn thing. Heading back to town now. I'm on I-71 about 50 miles out," Dave said calmly

"Are we still on for tonight," Marion asked as he looked at Liyah staring down at her phone.

"Of course. I'm a text you the location. Also I got 9 Pippen's from them thirty yellow bands Jay gave us," Dave said.

"Are you fucking serious? Nine Scottie fucking Pippen's for the thirty? Well I think you're going to need a bigger car; I just got off the phone with Jay and he got a hundred yellow bands for me to pick up tonight," Marion said as a drunk outside of B-n-M's knocked on his window asking for a few dollars.

"That's good for business. With that we'll be set from here on," Dave said blowing his horn at someone.

"So before I meet up with you I'm going to pick that up first. Oh shit I got to go, my P.O. seems like she's getting upset," Marion said chuckling as he rubbed Liyah's leg and she pulled away with a glare in her eyes.

"Ha ha ha....how's Liyah doing anyways? Tell her it's my fault and I'll make it up to her later," Dave said as the call ended and Marion started the truck.

Liyah sat quietly, mentally calculating what she just heard. *"Scottie Pippen meant coke so tote had to be the price,"* she thought while looking at her phone. She pressed the off button on her phone mentally playing the video back in her head. She felt her nipples through her shirt. With his conversation ended their destination…was the condo.

He looked at her and noticed that she was in deep thought.

"What you thinking about," Marion asked her.

"Nothing," Liyah responded as she thought of Deep Stroke's dick.

"Well, you got to be thinking about something. You're too quiet," he said.

"It's nothing, damn," she exclaimed out of frustration.

"Okay, fine fuck it! I was just trying to see what the fuck was wrong with your ass," Marion said getting upset.

Liyah stared out the passenger window trying to not let Marion fuck up her thoughts. They drove home in silence. They lived in the luxurious condominiums called The Drake. Marion barely pulled into their garage when Liyah stormed into the house. She didn't say a word. Marion walked in with the food and threw his keys on the end table.

He sat the food on the kitchen island. They both remained silent as they passed each other. Liyah went upstairs and changed into a t-shirt and boy shorts. Marion made their plates and walked into the living room.

When Liyah returned, she grabbed two beers and met him in the living room. She saw her plate and sat on the comforter. She said her prayer as she broke the tension.

> "I'm not upset babe. I just thought we would have dinner together that's all. I'm sorry," she said as Marion took a bite of his ribs.

He nodded in agreement. Through his sticky fingers, he blew her a kiss. Liyah turned on the TV and stopped at the 11 o' clock news. They were talking about the recent murder at Woodland Apartments. "Damn, I should call my cousin Bunchy. He stays over there," he said out loud. Their attention was drawn to Marion's phone as it vibrated on the glass table.

He licked the sauce from his fingers and noticed it was a text. Dave had written:

> "Meet me at US-271 by mile marker 115 in an hour. You'll see me," Marion scratched his head and texted his reply.

> "Ok, I'll be there but you fucked up my dinner. Before I get there get me a polish boy," he wrote.

Dave quickly replied, "I got you. I wouldn't have it any other way."

Liyah placed her plate in the sink. She finished her beer and tossed it in the trash. She knew the life that Marion lived; she despised his sporadic behavior. A part of her was upset that he was leaving; however, she knew she wouldn't be upset too long.

She turned the TV off and they headed upstairs. Marion explained for the thousandth time why he does what he does. She jolted as he held her from behind. He slowly kissed on her neck. The moment lasted no more than two minutes. Marion quickly went to the closet and changed clothes.

While Marion was talking, Liyah phone chimed with a message from Deep Stroke.

> "Girl I'm on my way…you better be ready," the text read.

> *"Marion will be leaving in the next few minutes. Every time he meets with Dave, he'll spend the night at some motel. So I'm good, everything should play out right,"* Liyah thought as she sat on the ottoman by their massive bedroom window.

The moon light shined through the parted drapes. She grabbed her notebook and ounce of OG Wyte Kush from her nightstand. Liyah sprinkled five grams into the blunt as Marion continued getting dressed. He finished getting dressed then sat on the bed in thought. She sat the tightly rolled blunt on her nightstand.

She placed her ounce and notebook back into the drawer. Through a bleak moment of silence, he stared at the floor and asked "Do you really love me?" Liyah just hugged him from behind and embraced him tightly. That gesture was enough to convince him of how she felt as he continued to gather his things.

Liyah phone chimed again with another message from Deep Stroke.

> "I'm here…I'm coming up," read the text.

She instantly got upset at the nerves of Deep Stroke she quickly replied.

"DON'T COME UP HERE YET! I'LL LET YOU KNOW. JUST SIT FUCKING TIGHT TILL I TEXT YOU BACK…"

He wrote "Fuck that nigga up there! Hurry the fuck up!"

Liyah didn't reply as Marion grabbed his wallet from the nightstand. He gazed at her from the other side of the room and said he loved her. Marion grabbed his overnight luggage from the closet. Liyah watched and admired the man she loved. He finished packing his bag then motioned for Liyah to come closer for a kiss. They kissed and embraced each other through the blaring of someone's car alarm. The car alarm agitated Marion as Liyah sat back on the ottoman.

"Baby look out there and see who's fucking car that is," Marion demanded

Liyah glanced through the drapes and became furious at what she saw. Deep Stroke was standing next to his gray Cadillac Escalade stroking his dick. He starred directly up at their bedroom window. She smiled slightly at the sight of Deep Stroke but was joggled back to reality. Marion demanded "Whose car is that, is it those new neighbors?" He quickly marched towards the window.

Liyah gently grabbed him by the crotch of his pants. She pulled him close before he could look out the window. "Baby calm down…ok," she said. He leaned down and kissed her as he grabbed her ass. She reassured him it was

nothing to such extremes. He kissed her as she told him it was the neighbor's car alarm going off.

Liyah let out a sigh of relief. *"If Marion would've seen this nigga outside! He would've killed him and me. Uggggh...what are you doing girl. Is this shit really worth it,"* she thought. He starred into his phone looking for available rooms at the downtown Marriott. He quickly booked a room and headed to the garage. He got into his truck kissed her goodbye and back out of the garage.

Chapter 1-2

Half an hour past since Marion had left the house. She checked her phone and saw numerous texts and missed calls from Deep Stroke. She texted him simply "Come up." Within moments, he knocked at the door. She prepared the bedroom for their usual tryst; she quickly trotted downstairs. She opened the door and cussed him out. He just leaned against the threshold sucking his teeth.

> "Look here…we agreed NOT to EVER get out of line with this! Don't disrespect me or my home especially when my man is here! Do you hear me! I'm doing you a favor," she screeched.

> He stood there quietly then suddenly grabbed her by the throat. "Now you listen to me? Don't you ever keep this dick waiting! Do I make myself clear," he demanded as he caressed her ass with his other hand.

Liyah agreed as he released her. She squeezed his dick and balls tightly. He moaned in submissive pleasure. "Do I make myself clear? I'm running the show," she uttered in a dominating voice as she released him. He headed to the bedroom as she locked the door.

> *"I'm going to bring the bitch out of him. He got some fucking nerves showing out…especially when my man is here! He gone eat everything I give him tonight,"* she thought as she walked to the bedroom.

Deep Stroke was looking out the bedroom window when she entered the room. She sat on the bed and lit her blunt. The pungent odor filled the room. Deep Stroke walked to the foot of the bed and stared at her. He quickly took his clothes off

and tossed them in the corner. The tattoo of his flamingo of death sat across his upper left shoulder with poise.

Liyah eyes swayed left to right watching his dick sway. She finished her blunt and edged closer to the foot of the bed. He looked down at her as he ran his fingers through her hair. She kissed the head of his dick and licked his balls. Liyah squeezed his ass while she sucked his dick. He flicked his fingers against his nipple rings.

She slurped back and forth along his 11 inches. The girth of his extremely hard dick filled her mouth. She felt the veins of his dick brushed against the roof of her mouth. When Deep Stroke shoved his dick down her throat saliva oozed from the corners of her mouth.

Liyah's head bobbed swiftly along his dick. She looked up at him while repositioning on her knees. Deep Stroke leaned his head back and moaned in pleasure. She reached up and squeezed his nipple as he played with the other. He gazed down at her with a stare of true sexual passion.

With his hand on her head, he rammed his long dick past her tonsils. She opened her throat then firmly slid two fingers deep into his ass. After few deep thrusts into his anus, she felt his dick pulsate in her mouth. He swung her head against the bed aggressively then heaved his dick into her bottomless throat.

> "Take this dick down your throat bitch! I'm about to cum," he grunted.

The surge of his semen shooting directly down her throat made her gag. Her eyes watered as he held her head in place against the bed. He slapped her across the face and demanded "You love this dick...don't you!" Deep Stroke's

semen always tasted sweet; she never minded swallowing for him. He held his dick down her throat till she swallowed every drop of semen.

He bent down and French kissed her as saliva and semen tangled in his goat tee. He reached down and flicked a finger across her moist pussy. She nudged back onto the bed sliding out her bra and panties. While he sucked on her neck she felt the warm saliva and semen smear across her skin.

Liyah eyes rolled as the euphoric feeling increased. He cradled her as her nipples and areolas hardened. He licked, nibbled and bit them as she rubbed his chest.

He slowly maneuvered the sensual kisses to her throbbing clit. The flick of his talented tongue made her body shudder sporadically as she gripped the sheets. She tried to scoot away but his firm hands held her in place. He gently massaged her thighs while he licked and suckled.

Her moans increased as her body shook and trembled. Deep Stroke knew she was about to cum; he stuck his tongue deep into her pussy. The sensation of his tongue combined with her euphoric feeling brought her to a breath taking halt. She climaxed in his mouth.

She felt the semen pulsate from her body. When she looked down, he rubbed his face against her now dripping pussy.

> *"She recalled when their affair began. He told her most women he'd been with don't like when he rubbed his face against their pussy. She's the first to actually enjoy it. Liyah loved Deep Stroke because she never had a freaky nigga like him. However, she wouldn't ever leave Marion. It was clear to her now*

why niggas have a main chick and a side bitch," she thought

His face was covered with cum as he kissed and licked her clit. He must've sensed her looking at him as he stared up at her intensely. He wiped his face with his hand as he licked the juices.

"Clean this pussy! I don't want to see a drop," she demanded as she held his head aggressively.

Before she could finish her statement, he flipped her over slapping her ass in the process. He immediately licked her ass. His tongue alternated between her pussy and ass as his finger rubbed her clit. Liyah reached on the nightstand for her vibrator and handed it to him.

He quickly placed it against her pussy while his tongue slid in and out of her ass. The rhythmic hum of the vibrator against her clit filled the room. The more Liyah panted and moaned the more aroused he became. He palmed her butt cheeks as he slid a finger in her ass.

Liyah arched her back and whined in pleasure. "Damn! I love it when you lift that ass for me," Deep Stroke said as he bit her butt. He buried his face back between her cheeks as Liyah gave orders. The sounds of passion throughout the room were shattered when her phone rang.

She glanced at the phone on the nightstand but missed the call. She checked and saw it was Marion. She presumed he's either leaving Jay's or heading to the motel. *"I'll talk to him tomorrow,"* she thought. During that momentary break, she opted to teach Deep Stroke a lesson about obedience.

"Umm...that felt so good," Liyah said as she pried Deep Stroke face from between her ass.

"Naah babe. What you doing? I'm not done yet," he complained when Liyah stepped off the bed.

"I'm not done either. Turn your ass around and bend over," she demanded reaching into the drawer on her nightstand.

Deep Stroke knew the routine. He quickly lubed his ass with the KY jelly. He was now on all fours with his ass propped in the air. Liyah focused intently on his ass while she put on her vibrating strap-on. Her black strap-on was 12 inches long and thick. He swayed back and forth waiting on her to initiate. Her nipples hardened from the anticipation of taking control.

> *"Every time they had sex, she thought about when she first fucked him. She always fantasized about trying dominatrix but never found a partner. Deep Stroke allowed her to fulfill that fantasy. The things they've done, Marion would never agree with but she loved their erotic spontaneous sexual relationship."*

She steadied his waist as she the black strap-on slid into his ass. He moaned as the 12 inches disappeared between his butt cheeks. The thrusting made his body twitch. She felt horny and excited as she watched the strap-on continuously pull and stretch his anus. He reached back and pleaded for her to slow down.

His pleas where ignored as she increased pace. Liyah was in a trance and became very aggressive. He looked back as if to speak but she smashed his face into the covers. *"You got some fucking nerves. Trying to show out because my man*

was home. Oh I got you," she thought while power thrusting in him.

She flipped him over on his back to look him in his eyes as she fucked him. He suddenly moaned loudly "I'm bout to fucking cum!" Immediately, the intense feeling she felt was on the verge of releasing. They both panted and gasped for air. She let out an orgasmic yelp as she rammed in him. He gripped the covers as stream after stream of semen shot from his dick.

A large blob of semen landed on his chest. She demanded him to eat it. He licked the semen from his chest. He held his massive dick and pointed at her. Two thick streams of semen landed on her abdomen and strap-on. They stared at each other as she slid out of his ass.

They laid there momentarily to catch their breaths. After about 10 minutes, she went to the bathroom and washed up. She walked back into the bedroom and plopped down on the bed. He signaled her to come lay down. She complied and didn't say anything. Within moments, she was in a deep sleep dreaming about what just happened.

Chapter 1-3

Meanwhile, Marion headed towards Jay's. He drove through Euclid Ave while passing through his old neighborhood. This was the quickest route to the outskirts of East Cleveland. He drove along a few twisting and secluded roads before arriving at Serpilla Fall.

The community glistened in the warm night against the clear moon light. Jay lived a simplistic life with his girlfriend Kimberlyn. Marion entered the security codes as the gates opened.

> *"Damn, my nigga is living the life. One day, me and Liyah will live like this,"* he thought pulling into their crescent shaped pebble stone drive way.

Marion immediately noticed Jay's new silver Mercedes S600 and matching hardtop convertible SL500. Next to his cars was Kim's pewter Audi Q7; however, Marion didn't see her black BMW 750IL. He figured she probably was working late since she was Senior VP of Milo Biotechnology.

Marion parked then walked up and rang the doorbell. Their custom built two-story home was gorgeous. The door opened and he was greeted by Kim who was now eight months pregnant. He kissed her softly on the cheek while rubbing her protruding belly. Marion and Kim were very close.

He held her hand as he escorted her to the living room couch. She quickly put her long shiny black hair into a ponytail. Kim's hair was very long due to her Native American roots. When she sat down, she placed her feet back into her hydro-massager.

"Where's Jay? Is he in y'all room or the den. Also, what time is it," Marion asked.

"Oh, he's in the den watching highlights of the game. It is a little after midnight. Now on to you mister, Liyah and I talked and she told me she's ready to be a mother," Kim said.

Marion stumbled over his words while she drizzled gravy on her baked potato.

"I don't think that we're ready for a child," Marion said as she shook her head and gave her blessings to them.

Marion was very fond of Jay and especially Kimberlyn. She was the sister he never had.

"Kim, where's your 750? I didn't see it outside," he asked.

"I traded it in for something new. Wait till you see what I got," she said as she finished her baked potato.

"Oh before I forget, are y'all coming to my baby shower in a few weeks? Also if you talk to Dave before me, tell him I'm going to hurt him badly for not stopping by in over a month. He can't be that damn busy! If Mya can make it over here at least twice a week then I knows his light skinned ass can," she retorted as he shook his head.

Marion finished talking and headed towards the den. He walked down their illuminated hallway. He always looked at their various childhood photos on the wall. There was a

picture of Kimberlyn crying with Santa Claus. It always made him laugh.

"I heard that! You would be crying to nigga. Or should I say Mari Mar Mar," Kim yelled from the living room.

"Look! Don't be cheating bringing up family nicknames and shit," he uttered loudly as she laughed.

At the end of the hallway was a short spiral staircase that descended to the den. Marion approached the door; he could hear Jay yelling in disagreement to an on field call. He walked in and sat down on the brown recliner next to Jay. There was a beer in the cup holder and he quickly cracked the seal.

"What's up nigga," Marion asked.

"Shit, trying to watch this fucking game. These bastards acting like they know I got $800 riding on them. They want me to lose my fucking money," Jay spat as another penalty flag is thrown.

"Mayne, why is Kim trying to pressure me into having a baby? Me and Liyah not ready for that just yet," Marion said as he sipped his beer.

"Nigga don't you think it's time for y'all to start a family. You know Kim sees you as her lil brother. She wants our baby to have a sibling or playmate," Jay said turning down the TV.

"I don't know. I'm not ready to settle down just yet," he said as Jay nodded.

Marion decided to call Liyah before it got too late. He saw it was 15 minutes after midnight and figured she'll be watching TV. His intentions of the call were to cuss her ass out for telling their business. She didn't answer the phone but he decided not to leave a message and just call her in the morning.

"Man, let me tell you. Why in the hell did Dave ask me to" Marion said before Jay interrupted him.

"I already know. He wants to meet at some odd ass place or in the middle of nowhere," Jay said calmly.

"Hell yeah, he wants me to meet him on US-271 by mile marker 115," Marion said in frustration.

"Mayne, that's Dave for you. He wasn't always like that though," Jay said focusing back on the game.

"What you mean," Marion asked as he lit his Black and Mild.

"Okay let me tell you, in the early 90's, there was this crew called the QMB. The Quincy Street Mob Boys. They ran the dope game in the late ninety's. Almost anything moving through Ohio was QMB affiliated.

They got caught up in a big fed bust. The niggas at the top of all that shit was Dave's father and his uncle Big Sleepy. I don't know what his father done but he got caught up in a murder rape case. The feds couldn't get his father to snitch but they still built their case against the QMB anyways.

The state and the feds sent their informants out looking for Dave's uncle Big Sleepy. One day, me and Dave had just left

Mi'Shele: Da Streets are Callin Me Pt. 1   page | 23

the casino. We pulled up to my house and noticed a black tinted Expedition and a white Jaguar where sitting in my driveway. We walked in the house and his uncle and two armed bodyguards were talking with Kim.

We all went to the den as he told us about the feds and the indictment. He gave me sixty-five thousand cash just for coming to my house. Sleepy told him that the white Jaguar outside was for him. He apologized for getting his father entwined with that murder.

Sleep said something about he was going to take a long vacation to get away. Then he and the bodyguards left in the black expedition. Me and Dave checked out the Jaguar and saw an envelope enclosed with a key in the glove box. There was an address attached to key.

Later that week, Dave went to the address which belonged to an investment bank. He told me the key was to a safe deposit box his uncle made in his name. The box held three things: a check for 500 thousand dollars, a piece of paper with a name and phone number and a picture of his father with his uncle.

If all that wasn't enough, DEA ran in Dave's mother house. They were serving a warrant pertaining to that QMB shit. They say his mother pulled a gun on an officer. During the shooting, his niece got shot and died instantly.

They say over 70 shots was fired. When it was all over, his mother and niece were dead. Rumors on the streets was Sleepy was dead and they was looking for his money. Me and Dave believed it cuz no one could find him.

We knew them pigs was lying, his mom's hated guns, so she definitely wouldn't keep one in her house. In turn, Dave took

most of his money and sued the DEA. They wound up settling for some undisclosed amount of installments over the next 15 years.

Their attorney was some smart mouthed bastard name Nathan Strokes. He swore there wasn't any wrong doing and promised justice wasn't served. After the case settled, Dave was like fuck everyone and everything. It's been like that ever since so that why he acts the way he does," Jay said as he sipped his beer.

Marion shook his head in disbelief to what he just heard. He noticed the ESPN post game show was coming on. The clock on Jay's wall read 12:47 am. *"It's about that time to be heading Dave's way,"* he thought. Jay told him the package was in his garage. They walked towards the living room as Kim sat there rubbing her belly.

Her foot massager droned out the sound of the TV. She insisted Marion give Liyah the child she wanted as he gave her a hug. Jay kissed her passionately on the lips then on her stomach. She inquired on what was they doing as Jay quickly replied "I have to show him my new lawn mower."

They walked into his illuminated garage which favored a car showroom instead of a garage. The garage was spacious and very clean. His laminated floor sparkled against the overhead lights. Jay walked over to a closet that was filled with boxes of diapers. He grabbed a box from atop a pile as he sat it on his work bench.

He opened the box and it was neatly lined with bundles of hundred dollar bills. Jay closed the closet and insisted Marion check out his lawnmower. Marion noticed that Jay wasn't concern at all about the money.

Mi'Shele: Da Streets are Callin Me Pt. 1   page | 25

"My nigga. I have to ask what's in this for you," Marion asked as Jay sat on the lawnmower.

"I want a secure future for my family. With what Kim and I make together we cool but Dave is the key," he said starring at the ceiling with his arms folded.

"I know with the 30 yellow bands I gave y'all, Dave probably got like 7-9 whole things back. Right now there's a drought in full effect. A whole thing in these streets is going for a minimum of 35k. I know niggas right now ready to buy soon as you drop that shit off to me," he said.

"So just imagine what he could do with that whole 100 piece. One thing I will say, Dave got the best plug in the Midwest. This in my opinion is the move I think he's been waiting to make," Jay said as he looked at a picture of him and Kim over his workbench.

"My nigga I got you. It's the same ole routine. After I pick that up, I'll be at the Marriott for the night. I'll hit you in the morning to pick it up," Marion said as he grabbed the box and headed to his vehicle.

Once he got situated in his SUV, he headed for the highway.

Chapter 1-4

After forty minutes of driving, there was a set of hazard lights blinking in the distance. He quickly merged over to the far right lane as he approached. It definitely wasn't Dave's white jaguar. Traffic was oddly sparse at this time of night. Usually, everyone's out cruising on warm summer nights.

He got closer to marker 115, he immediately noticed Dave's pearl white Jaguar on the shoulder. His hazards were blinking. Marion turned on his hazards and merged to the shoulder. Dave sat in a blue lounge folding chair in the grass next to his car. Marion parked ten feet behind Dave's white jaguar. He got out and walked closer. Dave sat coolly drinking a large Mr. Hero's fountain drink.

The rear of his car was jacked up with the rear driver side tire lying on the ground. *"He never fails to amaze,"* Marion thought as he looked at Dave. He could hear his car stereo since he stepped out his black SUV. The Isley Brothers was all he heard as Dave grooved to the music without a care in the world.

> "What's up? Why we had to meet all the way out here," Marion asked as they shook hands.
>
> "Well, you know me. You can't be too safe. Besides, Cuyahoga County is as good as any other. Gone head and pop a squat," Dave said as a semi sped past.

The breeze coupled with the warmth of the summer's air convinced Marion to take his offer. Dave quickly retrieved another folding chair from his trunk. Marion watched vehicles past bye as he sat in the chair. Dave handed him his

food. The mesquite aroma tingled his senses as he peeled back the silver foil exposing the plumped Polish boy.

"So what's the word? Let's get down to business," Marion said with his mouth full.

"This is the business. Do you know what this mean? This time next month we should be seating on at least four hundred thousand after we get these Scottie Pippen's off," he said in between sips calmly.

"Are you fucking serious! So you got nine of them whole things for the 30 yellow bands," Marion said staring at Dave in disbelief.

"I wouldn't lie. My uncle plugged me in decades ago. The main issue was timing and money," Dave said as he finished his drink.

"You're talking about you uncle Big Sleepy. Jay told me all about the QMB shit earlier. Nigga I didn't know them was your people. But if you don't mind me asking what really happened with your father," Marion said as Dave tossed his empty cup.

"Well, when I was eighteen my uncle, Big Sleepy and my pops controlled the QMB. The Quincy Street Mob Boys controlled all the cocaine that flowed through Dayton, Cincinnati and Cleveland in the late 90's. My pops is at Mansfield's doing life for a triple murder and rape.

My father, my uncle and some weak ass nigga named Stony went to confront some A-line runner down on Harvard Street. They ran in on the nigga to collect what he'd siphoned from the packages he delivered. They beat his ass

and dragged him upstairs. While they were upstairs his bitch walked in on the robbery."

They came downstairs with the 40k and saw this weak ass nigga raping the bitch. During their brief argument, the dude came from upstairs with a pistol and shot my uncle in the shoulder. My pops shot him and he bled out on the spot. He turned to kill the broad and Stony tried to spare the bitch.

Unc shot the bitch in the face then shot Stony. It wasn't until later that night they discovered that nigga didn't die. Unfortunately, Stony remained alive long enough to snitch on my father. He died two days later before he could tell on my uncle. The feds tried to indict my father on the three murders and rape.

"At that time, the feds where building a case against the QMB and wanted my father to snitch on Sleepy. He didn't cooperate so they recommended the state to take him to trail. He lost due to Stony's confession. The judge gave him life without parole and he's been at Mansfield ever since." Dave said nonchalantly.

> "Damn. That's some real nigga shit right there. But let me put that shit in my ride cuz I got to grab them 100 yellow bands anyways," Marion said as he walked to his vehicle.

Dave looked at him awkwardly as he held a colorful box labeled "Huggies." Dave laughed momentarily as they walked to the trunk of his white jaguar. Marion opened the box briefly as Dave peeked inside. He opened the trunk slightly which activated the hatch light.

From the illumination, Marion saw a large burgundy piece of traveler's luggage with a dark skinned guy bunched next

to the luggage. The stocky built man had a black burlap sack over his head. There were blood stains on his sky blue t-shirt and black shorts. He seemed to be restrained to the fetal position. Marion noticed the handcuffs on his wrist and ankles as he handed the money to Dave.

> "So, what's up with this nigga," Marion said as he pulled the burgundy bag from the trunk.

> "This nigga here wants to lie and steal from the hand that fed him," Dave said sarcastically.

> "Naah…I wasn't! I swear," the man pleaded as Dave demanded him to shut up.

> "Now you remember when we kept getting them packages that were short 2 and 3 ounces. Well this is the reason why they were. While I was handling business, my man tells me he found the snake behind our shortages. He paid the differences plus interest. So in good favor, he asked for me to dispose of this pest," Dave said as the man screamed for his life.

Dave walked to the passenger side of the car as he looked inside the center console. He returned with a Taser as he jammed it into the man's neck. The crackle of the Taser sent chills down Marion's spine. The man's body shook and shuddered as Dave let the voltage course through his body.

> "That should keep him quiet for a while," Dave said as he sat the colorful "Huggies" box in the trunk and closed it.

Marion put the large burgundy bag in the back his SUV with his overnight luggage. Dave put his tire back on his car. He quickly got on his phone and made a call. After about two

minutes of slight pacing, he smiled as he ended the call. "We need to go see "The Doctor," Dave said.

That meant only one thing…the guy in the trunk won't be alive for too much longer. Marion decided that he'll follow Dave to The Doctor's office. He opened the trunk as he threw the folding chairs in on top of the unconscious man's body.

Suddenly, a set of red and blue lights flashed in the distance behind Marion's SUV. The lights closed in as the police stopped and got out. Dave took his berretta from his waist and quickly sat it inside the car. Marion remained calm as he walked towards his black SUV. The highway patrolman approached as he asked "How y'all do tonight? Are you guys ok do y'all need any help?"

> "Naah officer. We're alright. We're just waiting on AAA." Dave said stepping from his vehicle.

The officer nodded as he gave a few words of safety. Dispatch came across his radio stating there was an accident a few miles ahead. He rushed back to his cruiser as he sped off. They watched his lights fade in the distance. They let out a sigh of relief as they got into their vehicles. Their destination was the Doctor's office.

Chapter 1-5

The drive to the Doctor's office took a little more than an hour. The Doctor was the owner and mortician for Miller & Bates Funeral Home. He was with the QMB but he put his money and skills to good use. Marion and Dave have done work with him in the past.

He done majority of the autopsies for Cuyahoga County. His funeral home obtained a ten year mortician contract with the Cleveland's Metropolitan Police Department. This in turn won him a three hundred thousand dollar company expansion grant. The city built an attached enclosed four thousand sq. ft. covered garage.

He had one of the best alarm systems money could buy.
The Doctor called Dave prior to them arriving. He told him the security code to access the garage. He also disabled the surveillance system momentarily by resetting the network.

He didn't want the cameras to capture Dave and Marion.
When they arrived to the rear entrance, they were met by a huge metal overhead door. Dave keyed in the code as the huge door came to life. It creaked and crackled as it lifted displaying the parking garage.

There were two plain white vans, three black limousines and three hearses. After they parked, Marion walked to Dave's car as he popped his trunk. The hooded man was motionless in the trunk. Marion removed his hood as they stared at his swollen blood clotted face. Marion noticed a steel gurney by the building's entrance. While Marion retrieved the gurney, Dave bludgeoned the man across the head with his tire iron.

"This for fucking with my money and fucking up my night," he spat.

Mi'Shele: Da Streets are Callin Me Pt. 1

"Calm the fuck down! Also your phone ringing," Marion said as he pushed the gurney.

Dave reached in his car and took the phone call. Marion heard him talking to his girlfriend Mya about why he'll be late coming in tonight.

He ended the call quickly as Marion positioned the gurney next to the trunk. They grabbed the man's bloodstained limp body and transferred him to the gurney. Dave closed the trunk as Marion watched the huge overhead door creak closed.

Suddenly, the man rose up and kicked Dave in his abdomen. He crumpled to his knees as he let out a high pitched shrill. Marion instantly grabbed him but struggled to maintain his grasp. The man quickly head butted Marion several times as he tried to flee.

He yelled and banged on the huge overhead door but to no avail. Dave regained his composure as his eyes fixated on the man. Dave observed that he had freed himself from his shackles. The man ran toward the building's entrance as he bumped into the Doctor.

The Doctor heard the commotion; he brought a syringe with him. He jammed it into the dark skinned man's chest. He slowly wilted and fell to the ground disorientated.
"Come pick this piece of shit up," the Doctor shouted.

They resituated the dark skinned unconscious man on the gurney, and then rolled him into the building. The Doctor led them through a corridor to a room labeled autopsy/incinerator. When Doc opened the door, the stench of formaldehyde and ethanol burned their eyes and throat.

Doc immediately activated the purge system to flush fresh air into the room.

Once it was clear to enter the room, they saw the freshly embalmed carcass at the center of the room. Doc calmly rolled the cadaver aside. He kindly pointed to where he wanted the dark skinned man. Dave walked slightly hunched over holding his stomach. They both took a seat while the Doctor prepared his tools on two metal trays.

The man was completely unconscious. Doc removed the man's ankle and wrist cuffs. He went to his office and returned with some restraints. He applied the leather restraints then sheared the man's clothing off.

The dark skinned man's eyes slowly opened and rolled around. He slowly regained consciousness as he groaned and grunted. The five point restraints held him tightly to the metal table. He wiggled his limbs but the restraints offered no slack.

Dave sat in a chair next to the cadaver locker. The bleak expression on his face displayed his concern. He said to Marion "I wondered how this nigga picked the locks on the handcuffs." Marion remained silent as he shook his head.

> "Hey Dave? Are you guys going to watch me work or y'all leaving," Doc said mixing chemicals by the sink.

> "Oh no...I have to see this bastard meet his maker," Dave ranted walking over to the dark skinned fellow.

Dave gazed the man up and down in disgust. "You're going to die today. It's going to be very slowly yet very painful,"

he said while the man pleaded for mercy. His loud voice reverberated off the white and grey walls.

"Shut the fuck up," yelled Dave in frustration. Doc finished mixing his concoction and started an I-V on the man. The bluish liquid flowed swiftly through the tube. "This will come in handy later," said Doc. Dave sat back in his chair; Doc began to work.

He grabbed a scalpel and began making incisions along the man's left foot and leg. He screamed in pain struggling against the restraints. Doc was focused because he completely ignored the shrieks. He made adjacent slices along his calf.

Dave now stood at the head of the gurney staring the man in his eyes. Through the screams there was a dull ripping sound. It was similar to carpet being pulled up. Marion got closer and saw Doc peeling back the skin on his left leg.
Doc saw the confused expression on Marion's face. "This is how it sounds when the epidermis is slowly separated from the tendons and muscles," Doc said over the man's horrible yells. He folded the skin up to an incision under the knee.

The man's body twitched and rippled with pain. Doc removed the creased skin and sat it on a nearby tray. The exposed ox blood red tendons contracted and expanded with every scream. He was being skinned from the waist down.

Within thirty minutes, the skin on the man's legs had been removed. The man ranted "I'll pay double please stop! Show mercy!" Dave poured alcohol onto the man's legs and watched his agony. He enjoyed every moment of his torture.

"Scream louder! Cuz this is really gonna hurt," yelled Doc making incisions along the man's face. Sweat trickled from

Doc's thick salt and pepper hair down his forehead. The man was in extreme agony. Doc gently flayed the skin from his face. He no longer had lips or eye lids to protect his eyeballs. Blood oozed from every direction of his face as the uncovered ligaments twitched and flexed.

Marion held his hand to his mouth trying to retain the vomit. Doc saw Marion and told him "If you're going to vomit aim it over here by the drain." He immediately hurled on the floor. Dave glanced at Marion with concern.

"Marion what's the matter with you? Your stomach upset or something," Dave asked over the shrieks of the dark skinned man.

"You're the damn problem Dave! We're not here to watch a nigga be tortured to death! If you're going to kill him do it already. We have other shit to be doing," Marion said kneeling over his vomit.

"Aight then fuck it...have it your way. Doc start the damn insinuator," Dave ordered looking at Marion sarcastically.

The man whimpered slightly knowing his death was imminent. It took two minutes for the insinuator to get to 1200 degrees. Dave leaned over and whispered in the man's ear. Doc rolled the gurney before the insinuator's heavy cast iron door.

"Doc unhooked one of his arms," Dave said eyes focused on the cast iron door.

"I don't think that'll be," Doc said before Dave interrupted.

"I don't pay you to fucking think! Just do what the fuck I asked you to do," Dave yelled.

Marion watched Doc release the leather strap restraining his left hand. The man gathered all his strength; removing the leather restraint from his head. Soon as he started on freeing his right hand, Dave opened the heavy cast iron door. Marion felt the intense heat from across the room.

"Now let me see you get out of this," Dave said as Doc pushed the gurney into the 1200 degree inferno.

The man's screams where still audible after Dave closed the cast iron door. Through the flame proof window, they watched the man incinerate. In ten minutes, the man's body was transformed into a mound of ash and ambers.

Dave went to his car to retrieve Doc's payment. Marion sighed as he rubbed his eyes. The sound of water striking the ceramic tiles filled the room as Doc hosed down the floor. Dave returned and handed him a small white envelope. Doc kindly stuffed it in his pocket.

"Whenever y'all need my services call me. Also, I'm about to reset to the system so by the time you guys get to your cars. Y'all will be in the clear," Doc said.

Marion didn't say anything to Dave. They walked to their vehicles in silence. Marion got in his black Porsche cayenne and waited for the huge overhead to rise. Once it rose, he zoomed out of the huge covered parking garage. Marion's sole focus was getting to his hotel room and lay down.

On his way to the Marriott, Dave called and apologized. Marion half-heartedly agreed, he thought about his warm hotel room and how tired he was. The drive to the hotel was short. He quickly settled in his executive suite and texted Dave and Jay.

"I'm at the downtown Marriott room 2415. I'll text y'all in the morning when I get up. It will be business as usual," he said setting his alarm before drifting to sleep.

Chapter 2-1

Mya opened the bedroom window letting in the night's breeze. The lace curtains fluttered in the breeze. The illumination from their lamps cast minor shadows on the wall. She sat on the edge of their king sized bed doing her nails.

"Babe have you seen my phone," Mya asked.

"I think you left it in the laundry room again. Matter of fact, mines is down there too. I'll get them when I get done," he said.

Dave was barely audible from inside their massive walk in closet. It was remodeled when they renovated their house. He converted it into a mini vault with reinforced walls and door.

When it took him this long in the closet, he's usually putting something in the floor safe. He appeared from the closet with a smile. "Close your eyes," he said with his hands firmly shut. She sat her nail polish on the nightstand. She grinned with anticipation. Dave opened his hand and revealed a small clear ring case. Before he could say a word she yelled "*yes!*"

He hugged her tightly as he twirled his fingers through her curly hair. The sound of their TV filled the room. She posed in the mirror with her beautiful gold diamond crested ring. "*He's finally ready to settle down,*" she thought. Suddenly, there was a loud crash downstairs.

The sound of wood cracking and glass shattering startled them. The house alarm blared; momentarily before the sound dissipated. "Someone is disabling the alarm," Dave thought while he ushered her towards the closet. Dave stood by the bedroom door listening intently. He heard numerous footsteps downstairs.

She wept and sobbed from the threshold of the huge closet. "I'm bout to give these bastards their issue! Lock the door and don't open it ok! You know what to do we've rehearsed this plenty of times," Dave told her with tears forming in his eyes.

Through his expression, she knew he was scared yet he remained confident. He pointed to the rack beside her in the corner as she handed him his Kevlar bulletproof vest. He uttered under his breath "thanks Mar." He thought about when Marion bought him the military grade body armor. He grabbed the M14 from the rack then kissed Mya. She knew what that meant as she shut the door and locked the cylinder.

The thunderous bursts of Dave's assault rifle reverberated through the reinforced walls. Each burst sent chills down her spine. The muffled sounds of yelling and screaming were inaudible as everything faded to black.

Liyah awoke from her horrible dream drenched in sweat and gasping for air. She looked frantically around the room as she rubbed her legs. There was an intense tingling between her legs. Deep stroke leaned away with a look of concern.

>"What's wrong? Did you have a bad dream? Do you want me to stop," he said to her.

>"Naah I'm ok. It was just a bad dream that's all. Don't stop," she told him as she guided his head back between her legs.

She felt her saturation which indicated she'd had an orgasm. He continued while she glanced at the clock. It read 6:49am. She let him proceed a few minutes longer before getting up to take a shower. The heat of the water began to condense on the shower glass.

Deep stroke observed her silhouette through the half frosted shower glass. Liyah's cogitation was immense. Her mind pondered over the significant of the dream. However, that thought was interrupted. "When are you going to leave him," Deep stroke demanded as she got into the shower.

> "We've been through this conversation numerous times. Please don't start today," she said looking over the shower glass.

He stood at the sink butt naked with his charming stare. The shower lasted about ten minutes. She quickly dried off and wrapped her black towel around her mid-drift. He leaned to kiss her only to be rejected.

> "Nate what's your problem lately," Liyah asked.

> "The woman I love is in love with another guy that doesn't treat her right. You know I treat u better than him. Obviously you're unhappy about something," he said pulling her close.

He kissed her neck as her eyes rolled in pleasure. The masculine grip of his hands on her shoulders sent pulses through her pussy. His erection was thumping against her ass. He whispered in her ear "I want to put all of this inside you."

She grinned while she entertained the thought. He slid his hand in the shower testing the warmth of the water. Liyah saw what he was doing and stopped him in his tracks.

> "What you doing Nate! You know we don't do that shit. It's bad enough we fuck on my man's bed but you're not washing your dick here. How many times do I have to tell you this," she exclaimed.
>
> "So I can't wash my ass," he barked.
>
> "You know that we don't do that. Why you acting brand new," she said nonchalantly.

She walked from the bathroom back to the bedroom. Nate observed intently as she grabbed her panties from the dresser. He watched her glistening body from the bed.

> "So it's ok to fuck me in his bed! But I can't wash my dick off," he exclaimed.

Liyah ignored him as she took the towel off. Nate looked at her with hopes for an answer with a coy expression on his face. She ignored his stare and grabbed her olive colored pant suit from the closet. Nate jumped from the bed and grabbed her arm and pulled her closer to him.

> "You don't hear me? You need to answer me when I'm talking to you," he said aggressively.
>
> "Don't get yourself hurt. Let go of my arm Nathan. I'm trying to get ready for work," she said glancing at her arm as he released it.

"Ok babe damn. You know how I feel about you. However, do you want to do lunch later," Nate said as Liyah's phone ranged.

Deep stroke grabbed her phone off the nightstand.

"Who is it babe," she asked.

"It's that nigga u love so much, he said sarcastically.

"Well, can you hand it to me?" Liyah asked putting on her blouse.

He tossed her phone on the bed; she looked at him and chuckled.

> *"I know this nigga is not mad. He knew that I had a man when I met him. Fuck him, that's his problem if his feelings get in the way. I'm not really trying to hear this shit,"* she thought.

She glanced at the screen flashing Marion. *There was a warm feeling as she answered the phone. Marion always made sure to call her before she left for work. This was his routine especially, when he would be handling business.* She sat at the foot of the bed as she tried to focus on her conversation. Nate flashed his long chocolate dick from across the room.

He slowly came and stood in front of her caressing his massive engorged dick. Liyah couldn't resist wrapping her lips around his swollen dick. She mumbled in agreement to Marion's questions. Deep stroke grinned as he came on her face.

His semen erupted from his dick landing on her lips, cheek and phone. She relished in the warmth of his thick semen before ending the phone call. She took her hand and wiped her face while glaring up at Deep stroke. She licked his semen from her manicured fingers.

She sucked the head of his dick collecting every drop of semen. He got dressed as he switched the conversation.

> "So what do you think the outcome of your case will be, "he said putting on his t-shirt.

> "I don't know. I think we have a good chance of a not guilty verdict. In my opinion," she said.

> "Well when you get done with trial, we'll get a bite to eat," he said before heading downstairs.

> "Ok that sounds great," she said gathering her things following him downstairs.

She watched Deep Stroke get into his gray Cadillac Escalade and speed away. She adjusted her seatbelt as the hardtop retracted on her Audi TT. The morning sun warmed the sky as she headed for downtown Cleveland.

Chapter 2-2

Marion's alarm sounded at 7:15am sharp. He got up and washed his face and brushed his teeth. He called Liyah and she answered on the third ring. She sounded delightful as she listened to his ranting.

The call didn't last long; she had to finish getting ready. He looked around his spacious and luxurious hotel suite. From the 22nd floor, he had a wonderful view of Cleveland's skyline. The burnt orange glow of the morning sun filled the skyline at 9:28am.

"Ding, ding, ding," sounded the chime signaling the whirlpool was full. He sat in the warm water and let the hydro jets work their magic. His mind recalled everything that had occurred within the past two weeks. He knew something had to give. Thoughts ranged from Liyah wanting to have a baby to Dave trying to make a cool million from the dope game.

The thoughts of settling down and raising a family were beginning to take center stage. However, Marion knew maintaining a family would be difficult. He saw his mother struggle from check to check through his entire childhood. That way of living wasn't for him. In a couple of months, he could easily bring home a hundred thousand.

Quitting now wasn't an option. Marion's loyalty to his comrade meant till the death. His phone vibrated on the nightstand but he knew it was most likely Jay. He savored the last moments in the whirlpool before getting out and drying off.

He looked at his phone and the text read "I'm pulling into the garage. I should be up there in 10 minutes." Marion threw on a black LRG t-shirt and some black and turquoise shorts. There was a knock at the door. A soft feminine voice said "room service." Marion forgot he ordered a large pizza forty minutes ago.

He tipped the lady and sat the pizza on the living room table. Shortly after room service left, Jay knocked on the door. He brought his usual black tote and a six pack of Corona's. Marion bit a slice of pizza while opening his burgundy traveler's case.

Marion sat a 9x9 block of cocaine on the table. Jay handed him a small white respirator "put this on cuz this looks real potent" he said. Jay put on a pair of thick latex gloves after he set up the digital scale. Next to the scale was a Pyrex beaker and vials of different acids which where to test the purity of the coke.

> "How was the meeting with D," Jay asked placing a respirator over his mouth.
>
> "Mayne...First off" Marion said rubbing his temple in frustration while summing up his meeting with Dave.
>
> "Well you can't put anything past D. They don't make them like him anymore. He's true and loyal to the rules of the streets," Jay said pulling out a little pocket knife.

He slit the top and dug a little out with a teaspoon. He dumped the teaspoon in a clear liquid which quickly turned dark blue. He in turned siphoned the blue fluid into another beaker with a yellow thick gel. It resembled jelly. The gel solidified and began to vaporize.

"Have y'all decided on any names yet," Marion asked watching the vapors rise from the beaker.

"I don't know yet. We're going through names at this point," Jay said swirling the beaker till the gel completely vaporized.

Jay nodded in agreement with Marion as to the product's potency. They often wondered who supplying Dave. Cuz no one in the state of Ohio had shit this pure. Jay closed the package and weighed the eight remaining bricks.

He sat them on the table; Marion placed them back into the burgundy case. Jay calmly placed the beakers and scale back in their tote. Jay grabbed a beer from the six pack and a slice of pizza. He walked to the window and admired the view.

Jay's phone rang; he uttered "it's Quintana." He answered the phone and simply said "I'll call you later with a time and location." He sat the phone down and finished his beer. Marion sat on the plush love seat devouring the pizza.

"You want to ride with me nigga," Jay asked coolly.

"Naah. I'm about to run some errand then go see my cousins Wow Wow and Bunchy. I'll link up with you later," Marion said while in deep thought.

"Oh ok. Tell them I said what's up," Jay said grabbing a slice of pizza and a beer for the road.

Marion grabbed the case as Jay held his black tote. He called Quintana and told him "location and time." Marion went to the bedroom and put on his Kevlar vest. Marion never traveled without it. They exited the room destined for the parking garage.

The elevator ride was brief as they stopped at sub level 2. Jay's silver S600 was parked across from the elevators. He popped the trunk as they approached the car. They plopped their cases in the trunk and closed the hatch.

Marion strolled to his black Porsche Cayenne then chucked the deuce. Jay acknowledged. They both exited the garage heading opposite directions.

Chapter 2-3

The drive to her downtown office was always tranquil; today was different. When she approached the center of downtown Cleveland she noticed the traffic around the Hall of Justice was gridlocked.

After a ten minute detour, she arrived at her law firm. Morris, Yarborough and Payne were deemed the second best private law firm by the mayor of Cleveland. Her office sat adjacent to the Hall of Justice. When she pulled into her curbside parking spot, she noticed her business partner Marsha outside smoking.

>"How's your morning going," Marsha said while blowing her smoke in the air.

>"It's alright. I'm just getting the day started," she replied still tasting Nate's semen in her throat.

She put on her blazer before grabbing her purse and briefcase. Liyah waved to Mr. Williams before getting out of her car. He owned William's Bond and Notary which was their next door neighbor. Liyah quickly retrieved a cigarette from within her briefcase and sparked the Kool menthol 100.

>"It's alright. We've left the Harlow file on your desk. We've highlighted all the questions for cross-examination and inconsistencies in the depositions," she said.

>"Alright thanks Marsha. So how do you feel the Jenson case," Liyah said taking a puff from her cigarette.

"Forget the Jenson case, how do you feel about the verdict today. What do you think the outcome will be," Marsha asked.

"Well I hate that they wanted to get started today at noon. Secondly, all the media attention over the air, I hope that it goes well," Liyah said, taking another puff.

"Well, I think that the verdict is going to get not guilty. The evidence doesn't add up." Marsha said.

Liyah looked at her watch and seen that the time is close to time to go to court. She mashed her cigarette against the city hall building. Marsha did the same and they both walked into the dark brown doors.

Her walk to the Hall of Justice was daunting. Traffic was gridlocked because of every media syndicate from Ohio to Illinois was following the story. Outside the hall of Justice was packed. This wasn't including protesters and demonstrators.

She was immediately swarmed by the media wanting insight as to her opinion of the trial. People protested their opinions about her client. Through steel will she bypassed the crowds and entered the building.

The lobby of the hall of justice was brimming with people this warm summer morning. Liyah's mind began to race in different directions. She wondered did her client know that his girlfriend and teenage son had been murdered last night. The motive was apparently clear; the words "Take from us! We take from you!" was written on the wall. The police immediately placed a gag order on the media until the outcome of the trial. The thought still baffled her yet the only answer was retaliation.

The elevator ride to the 17th floor was quick. She logged in at the clerk's office as she requested to speak with her client. Derek who was the bailiff of the courtroom escorted her back to the holding cell. Liyah always knew that Derek found her attractive.

> "Hey Ms. Morris. How was your night last night," he asked walking beside her.
>
> "Hey Derek, my night was good, how about yours," she replied.
>
> "It was okay, would have been better if you was in it," he said flirtatiously.

Liyah blushed at his remark. She then started to chuckle as they continue to walk down the hallway.

They opened a brown door which concealed the holding cell area. There were two men in orange jumpsuits pacing when she entered. Her client was a young nineteen year old on trial for a triple homicide. He stood in the corner gazing through the small window.

Derek yelled his name which broke his concentration. His eyes glistened at the sight of Liyah standing before him. She noticed how the dress shirt and slacks improved his visual demeanor.

> "Hello Mr. Johnson. I see that the shirt and shoes worked out for you," she said.

"Oh yeah. I like your style. So what is the verdict looking like," Mr. Johnson asked rubbing his sore handcuffed wrists.

"Well, so far the evidence has been looked at and we are waiting on the jurors," Liyah said.

"Well, I guess we'll see justice prevail," Mr. Johnson said buckling his pants.

"Look, I know this is hard for you. I'm getting you out of here. You have to trust me," she said.

Liyah quickly marched back to the courtroom and prepared her things. This case was so high profile that three prosecutors decided to take the case. They wanted the maximum which was 60 yrs. with no option for parole. She decided to take the case pro-bono to increase the company's well maintained image.

She noticed the prosecutors where conversing amongst themselves in a small huddle. Mr. Johnson's mother sat in the back with tears forming in her eyes. Liyah walked past her client's family out into the lobby to get a breath of fresh air.

She was once again swamped by the media as well as the victim's family. She politely declined any statements as family members displayed pictures of their deceased loved ones. She remained silent focusing on the task ahead.

Derek stuck his head out of the double doors. He motioned for Liyah and the victim's family to enter the courtroom.
The news' anchors wrapped up their stories as Liyah walked into the courtroom. The tension was very thick as she headed

to her table. There were three additional sheriffs in case any family members got too hysterical.

The judge banged his gavel and called the court to order. Liyah and the prosecutors stood silently as the defendant entered the courtroom. The once promising Kent State youth was now reverted to a scared fearful child vying for his freedom. The victim's family moaned and groaned displaying their distaste towards the defendant.

In turn, Mr. Johnson's family sobbed showing their sympathy. The front row of the courtroom was a brood of anguish, confusion and sorrow. The tension was intensified once the presence of the twelve jurors entered the courtroom.

Everyone took their seats and watched the judge fumble with his glasses. He turned the floor over to the prosecutors for closing statements. Liyah rolled her eyes as the big mouth new prosecutor took the floor.

"To the jurors, before you decide on your verdict, think about the victims. The victims' families, the victims' friends and all the heartache caused by Mr. Johnson. Now if y'all don't remember I'll refresh your memories.

On the night in question, Mr. Johnson and some of his friends decided to go to a party. They had a few drinks too many and got put out the party. One of Mr. Johnson friends gets into an argument with some guys.

While Mr. Johnson was leaving the party, a fight broke out. While the defendant was seated in the rear passenger seat, a witness stated she saw the defendant friend lean out the window holding a long black gun.

Bang, bang, bang until the magazine was empty. Now what society do we live in that decides to ride with friends and shoot up parties? He's just as guilty as the person who pulled the trigger. Over 30 spent casings were recovered from the scene.

Whether he knew or didn't, the defendant failed to inform law enforcement. So we ask you today to find him guilty. No more your honor", the prosecutor said walking in front of the juror's bench.

The judge nodded in agreement while looking at the defendants table. Liyah didn't have a rebuttal because there was insufficient evidence to support their claims. Instead, she waved her option for a closing statement. One of the bailiff's stood next to the foreman who handed him a slip of paper.

"Your honor I believe the jury has reached a verdict," he said.

The defendant leaned over and whispered to Liyah "I really need to use the restroom.

"Excuse me your honor. May my client use the restroom please," she asked as the judge put the court at recess for 10min.

The bailiff escorted Mr. Johnson back to the holding cell to use the restroom. Liyah sat patiently as the clocked ticked away. The recess pasted slowly. The bailiff went to get the defendant then all hell broke loose.

The sheriffs' radios blared continuously "10-54A! Need medical attention to 17th floor HC 4!" The bailiffs ran from the courtroom to rear entry hallway. Both families looked on confused. The families began to get hysterical so the judge banged his gavel yelling "order, order!"

Liyah ran from the courtroom to the holding cell. Immediately, she noticed the young man's body dangling from the ceiling vent. Two officers supported his body while another cut his make-shift noose. He had apparently hung himself with his tie. One officer tried CPR while another questioned the convicts in the cell

> "What the hell happened in here," yelled an officer looking around the holding cell.
>
> "I don't know. He just said he can't deal with this shit any more. He said he didn't do it and it's not fair. That's what he said," a convict said pointing to the TV.
>
> "Why did y'all didn't stop him. I could charge y'all with accessory to a suicide," stated the questioning officer.
>
> "That's not my problem," the convicts retorted.

Everyone in the cell glanced at the TV and saw the broadcast. Liyah mouth dropped upon seeing the news story. She was sure the gag order was in effect. Yet, someone on at the news station definitely dropped the ball.

> *"Mr. Johnson's girlfriend and son were found slain in their apartment last night. We do not know if this is directly tied to Mr. Johnson's case; however, today the jury will return with a verdict.*
>
> *We do not know if the murder of Mr. Johnson's girlfriend and child will impact the juror's decision.*

We are waiting on the outcome. Police isn't giving many details but we will keep you posted on this developing story," said the TV news anchor.

Liyah stood out the way of the EMT's. She starred in disbelief at the young man's lifeless body. The EMT's used their defibrillator three times to no avail. They couldn't get a stable pulse he was declared DOA.

She walked slowly back into the courtroom which was in a frenzy. The judge regained control and demanded the foreman to read the verdict. Each family fell silent. Everyone's eyes were glued on the foreman.

> "Your honor the jury has reached a unanimous decision. We find the defendant....not guilty," he said.

The judge quickly relieved the jurors of their duties. The bailiff ushered them down the hallway behind the courtroom. He sighed heavily placing his glasses on the bench.

> "Now to all the families this verdict reflects the opinions of your peers. So don't take this as your loved ones death not being avenged. Now to the defendant the outcome may be victorious; however, during the recess the defendant hung himself. Our medical team wasn't able to revive him. So to you all, I send my condolences," stated the judge

The courtroom erupted. Sheriffs swarmed in and quickly cleared the feuding families. One of the victim's brothers' wanted to fight. "What's happening? We right here," he yelled. Liyah collected her notes and paperwork and stuffed them into her briefcase.

The court reporter looked around at the chaos within her courtroom. The judge drank a glass of water as he tried to regain control. His reddened face held an expression of frustration. He took a deep breath and spoke loudly.

The rapture ceased momentarily.

> "We wanted to preserve the integrity of the trail," the judge said sternly four times.

He quickly disappeared to his chambers. The prosecutors gathered their things and asked one of the bailiffs to escort them out of the courtroom.

The Defendant's mother fainted at the thought her son was dead. The EMT's returned to provide treatment. Liyah slide out of a side exit down an adjacent hallway. When she exited, she was on the far side of the 17th floor lobby. She saw the media swarming the feuding families for an exclusive interview.

"When I took this profession I didn't sign up for this," she thought rubbing her eyes waiting on the elevator. The emergency elevator doors opened and three EMT's appeared. They were pushing a stretcher towards the courtroom. The news anchors filmed every moment.

The ruckus was loud. When Liyah got onto the elevator the two families began fighting in the courtroom lobby. When the doors closed, she had a brief moment to think. She felt bad because he hung himself with the tie she gave him.

Word traveled fast about the commotion on the 17th floor; other people boarded the elevator destined for the 1st floor speculated about what just occurred.

Chapter 2-4

Her phone vibrated in her pocket as the elevator reached the first floor lobby. It was a text from Deep Stroke. The message simply stated "meet me at Sidewalk Café at 1:30pm." She walked outside and glanced up at the huge clock on the side of the Tower City building.

She had forty minutes to spare. "It's so sunny outside. I need to get to some air anyways," she thought walking to her office. Sidewalk Café was very popular amongst lawyers.

When she walked into the bistro, she spotted Nate sitting at a white clothed table. He greeted her with a kiss and warm embrace. They took their sits and glanced at the menus. Nate sipped his water while Liyah skimmed the menu.

"I hope this nigga don't talk about this morning. I don't have time for that jealous shit right now. After the day that I just had, I can't take it. I got to stop fucking with him," she thought as Nate got her attention.

"Liyah, hello! You going to answer my question," he asked.

"I'm sorry, what did you say?" Liyah asked.

"What was going on up on your floor today? I heard they found a dead body," Nate said.

"Yeah, that was my client. He hung himself and I feel horrible. Also what makes it worse is the verdict was not guilty," she said sadly.

"It'll be alright. However, let me excuse myself. I need to use the restroom. I'll be right back," Nate said.

Liyah took a sip of her drink and shuttered when someone sternly tapped her shoulder. She nearly choked when she looked over her shoulder. *"Oh my fucking god! What the hell is Kim doing here,"* she thought before replying.

"Kim! What you doing here," Liyah said looking speechless.

"Hey girl, I'm here meeting with some investors that want to know about the company. What you doing here." Kim asked while Nate walked up.

He kissed her on the cheek passionately then took his seat. Liyah looked at Kim and immediately felt ashamed. "She going to tell Marion everything," she thought. Kim held a firm poise ignoring what she saw.

"What you doing here girl," Kim asked.

"Oh, I'm just having lunch with my co-worker, Nate," she said as Nate shook Kim's hand.

Kim excused herself as her investors had arrived. She pulled her phone out and quickly texted a message before leaving.

Liyah's mind was racing. She really didn't know that to say or to think.

Her phone vibrated and she knew instantly it was from Kim. The message said "Meet me in the restroom NOW." She feared what Kim would say or think. *"Is she going to tell what just happened? I hope she don't think I don't love*

Marion. Will she understand? Why am I doing this," she thought emotionally.

She watched Kim walk across the floor with a purpose. Liyah steadied her beliefs and confidence and went to the restroom. Kim stood by the mirror with her arms folded with a scolding expression. Her face displayed disappointment and frustration.

"Okay, what you want to know," Liyah said sniffling and opening her heart.

"Are you cheating on Mar," Kim demanded.

She agreed and Kim shook her head in disagreement.

"What the fuck Liyah! Why would you do this to him? Marion is a good man and he treats you good," Kim stated while rubbing her stomach.

"Honestly...I feel Nate deep in my soul. He takes me to the places we women fantasize about. Marion doesn't take me there anymore," Liyah said glancing at the mirror.
"What! Listen to yourself! All he's giving you is some dick Liyah! Take it from me that man out there isn't worth losing your relationship," Kim said emotionally.

"Kim, it's too much to explain right now. What are you doing later, I'll tell you about it tonight," Liyah said.

"I'll be free this evening. Also Jay's going to be out so it'll just be us. Just call me when you're on your way," Kim said washing her hands.

They left the restroom and went to their tables. Liyah approached her table and thought *"maybe I should call this affair quits."* Nate's charming ways swayed her differently as he cleaned his ring with his tie. He was such a gentleman.

Their food had arrived and he hadn't touched his plate because he was waiting for her to return.

> *"Tonight is not going to be fun. Uggh this shit isn't cool. Well she knows now so I might as well tell her everything. I hope she understands,"* Liyah thought jokingly glancing at her plate.

Chapter 2-5

Once lunch was done it was back to reality. She went back to her office. Marsha was at her desk making notes on a case file. Liyah looked exhausted and Marsha sensed it.

She gave her a heartfelt embrace. Her moral lifted slightly. Liyah went to her office and checked her messages. The secretary left notes atop her briefcase on her desk. Marsha sat in the chair in front of her desk as Liyah hung up her suit jacket.

> "What's going on? Are you ok? I heard what happened in court," Marsha stated.

> "I'll be okay. Just don't want to talk about it. I have to focus on something else that's all," Liyah said.

> "Ok. We'll I was looking over the Miltonberry case. This one is kicking my ass. Prosecutor Guzman wants to add Possession of a Controlled Substance II and enhance the first count of possession to dealing," Marsha said rubbing her eyes in frustration.

Marsha's phone rang in the other room. She politely excused herself and closed Liyah's door. Liyah looked over her secretary notes. One note stated, the media wanted an interview with Mr. Johnson's attorney about why he committed suicide.

She slipped the notes into her briefcase and checked her email. Her partner Keith Yarborough sent an email asking type up Motion of Change of Venue. She quickly began working his motion. Suddenly, her phone chimed with a text from Kim saying "What time will you be here?"

She glanced outside and saw the burnt orange glow of the setting sun. "Damn where did the time go," she thought applying the finishing touches to Keith's motion. Liyah turned everything off in her office. To her surprise, Marsha had already left.

There was a note on the bulletin board "Didn't want to disturb you. See you tomorrow." She armed the security system. Her phone rang as she walked to her car.

"Hey baby I missed you. What you been doing," Liyah said with excitement in her voice.

"I missed you too. I've was handling business as usual. Also Jay stopped by and we just talked. I'm driving right now though," Marion said.

"Oh ok, where are you going and are you coming home tonight," she asked.

"I'm heading over my cousin Bunchy's house. His lil brother Wow Wow just came home today and they're celebrating. So, I don't think I'm going to be home but I'll let you know before the night's end," Marion said turning down the radio.

"Well I'm not going to keep you, just call me later babe. I love you, Liyah said.

Chapter 2-6

When Marion pulled into Woodland apartments he just got off the phone with Liyah. It was 8:30pm and Bunchy stayed in the most ratchet, crime infested and dilapidated complex in the city. Within the last six days, two people were gunned down in the apartments. The notorious reputation of Woodland didn't stop Marion; because he lived here as adolescence.

He pulled up to Woodland's entrance and 3/4's of the security gate was lying on the ground. It appeared someone recently drove through the gate. All the hood rats and boppers in the complex were out walking this evening. Immediately, everybody's attention was on Marion's SUV, especially the jealous niggas.

Marion followed the road straight around the bend. Bunchy's apartment was on the left; Marion pulled into the parking spot. Bunch was Wow's older brother. They were his Aunt Pam's boys.

Wow Wow's baby momma was outside watching the grill and talking with friends. Marion sat in his truck as the people stared in awe. When he stepped out, she recognized him immediately. She told him "Wow's down there shooting dice."

This was a release party for his little cousin Wow Wow. He just came from doing 6 straight at Richland Correctional Institute. There was numerous banners and placards throughout the apartments saying "Welcome home Wow Wow." This was ghetto love at its finest.

The aroma of barbeque filled the air from the four grills. The females on the porch whispered amongst themselves.

Marion heard the snickering about his looks, physique and truck. He smiled and downplayed the compliments.

Marion pulled up a seat waiting on Bunch and Wow. Wow's baby momma made him a plate. Bunch parked his aqua blue box Chevy next to Marion's black SUV sitting on 24 inch Arelli's. Bunch hopped out instantly noticed Marion on the porch.

>"What's the fucking bizz," Bunch said hugging Marion.
>
>"Long time no see Bunch. How have you been," Marion said chuckling.
>
>"I've been quite alright. I'm just trying to get up there on your level. However, I see you still wearing that hard ware," Bunch said tapping Marion's vest.
>
>"You know me. I can't leave home without it. You know what goes on in these streets," Marion said lifting his shirt displaying his Kevlar vest.

A small group of thugs walked up to Bunchy's house. A couple of them didn't have shirts on; one had his pistol on his hip; while a few others were counting money. A guy walked up that he didn't recognize. Turned out, Wow had grown dreads and a beard.

Bunch looked in the cooler and saw that they were almost out of liquor. Wow saw the expression on Bunch's face as he slammed the cooler lid. Wow offered to get the drinks as he kissed his baby momma. Bunch tossed him the keys to his aqua colored box Chevy.

"Hey Cuz, you going to ride with me to the liquor store," Wow said drinking the last sip of his Seagram's gin.

"Shit alright. We got to talk anyways," Marion said getting into Bunch's car.

Wow started the car as the wang from the bass shook the ground. "Damn that shit slapping," Marion thought. He laughed at his little cousin because he was so excited to drive the car. He quickly reversed out and sped towards the liquor store.

"Damn Cuz let me tell you about this shit! I didn't get a chance to tell you cuz shit got crazy when the case happened," Wow said.

"Tell me about it. I never did get all the details," Marion said turning down the music.

"The night it all went down, me and Ty was chilling over this bitch house. We didn't know she was Peezy's girl. Ty was going to fuck her while I get her friend. We was smoking and drinking and he kept blowing up her phone.

So the nigga came to her house and start banging on the door. Me and Ty wasn't worried cuz we both had a tool on us. Ty chose to leave. We grabbed our smoke and walked out the door.
Peezy started talking shit. It was about 5 of them. It popped off when Ty walked past and somebody punched him. One of them up's a pistol then Ty started dumping.

His shit jammed then we ran towards my car. So in the heat of the moment, I let off three rounds. Unfortunately, one of the rounds hit Peezy in the face. His niggas ran and we dipped out.

The only thing that placed me on the scene was my car. I didn't know the apartment's had surveillance. Then a couple days later,

I was downtown charged with murder. They wanted me to snitch because they really wanted to pin the case on Ty.

Since I didn't co-operate, they took me to trial. They couldn't convict me of murder. Yet they found me guilty of involuntary manslaughter." he said while waiting at a red light.

"But here's when shit got real. The first night my cell mate tried to kill me! I was sleep. I woke up with two niggas trying to hold me down while my cell mate stabbed me.

I got free and wrestled the banger from that nigga. Meanwhile, the other two where punching and kicking me. I stabbed one of them in the face and the other in his neck. Guards heard the commotion and broke it up.

Two weeks later is when you came to visit. Give Dave my props; he's a real nigga! When you said you'd holla at him, he came through. I went from the most hated to the most feared.

The money y'all put on my books had me feeling like I was the Don. I don't know how Dave did it but he definitely had some pull and power," Wow said.

Marion nodded in agreement to Wow's statement.

However, his attention was focused on this red dirty SUV that had been following them since they left the apartments. The dirty SUV parked on their driver side when they pulled up to the liquor store. Three guys got out and followed Marion and Wow. The driver wore a red fitted hat with the initials MVB, which stood for Murder Ville Blood.

The other had a dread mohawk while the third guy had gold in his mouth. They walked in after Wow with one of them sporting a dread mohawk bumping into Marion. He held his tongue in sake of keeping the peace. The guy with dread mohawk mumbled something that Marion dismissed. Wow was oblivious as he darted into the store.

They stood at the cooler deciding on which beer; Miller Draft or Bud Light. One of the guy's stares caught Wow's attention. Marion whispered to Wow "Be cool alright. I'll handle this okay." They grabbed two 24-packs of Bud Lights and headed to the counter.

> "What the fuck you keep looking at bitch ass nigga," said one of the guys.

> "Nigga you ain't saying shit," Wow said aggressively stepping up to their clique.

> "My bad nigga. He be tripping at times," said the guy in the fitted hat in a shady voice.

Marion paid for the drinks as they headed to the car. Wow placed the bags in the back. They sat in the car briefly talking before putting the car in gear. The guy with dread mohawk leaned out the passenger window of their SUV and signaled Wow. He rolled the window down.

> "Ah my nigga is your name G-Child. You look familiar," said the guy with the dread mohawk looking shifty.

> "Fuck naah my nigga! They call me Wow Wow," he said sarcastically rolling up the window.

Marion told him he had almost got into it with one of them niggas. Wow laughed at the thought of his big cousin fighting somebody. Wow began backing out when the passenger doors opened on the suv. Then the passengers of the suv got out and opened fire on their car.

Mi'Shele: Da Streets are Callin Me Pt. 1   page | 68

"This for Peezy weak ass nigga," the guy with the gold's yelled angrily.

People scattered in different directions escaping the mayhem. Wow mashed on the gas and the car began to sputter. Marion ducked down directing Wow to get to the other side of the lot. They could hear the bullets grinding and boring into the car. "Agggh I'm hit," Wow screamed in agony slumping on Marion's shoulder.

The car overheated then cut-off. Marion saw the steam and smoke coming from the engine compartment. They slowly rolled into a concrete light pillar. Marion glanced behind them and saw the shooters jogging toward the car.

Marion frantically pulled Wow out the passenger door. He was definitely hit: Marion couldn't see the wound due to all the blood. Wow Wow grimaced in agony from every subtle movement. Marion looked under the car and saw the shooters footsteps getting closer.

"Nigga we been waiting on you! You think we gone let you slide? You killed my nigga Peezy! It's time to die today," yelled one of the shooters.

Marion remembered that Bunch rides like him. He always kept old school Chevys' because he could hide his guns under the back seat. Marion opened the rear passenger door and fumbled with the seat. The darkness of the night complicated things. He slid his hand under the seat and felt nothing.

The rear window shattered raining shards of glass and debris atop Marion's head. He rubbed his hand against the back of his neck and head and noticed he was bleeding. Before he could locate the wounds, bullets whizzed by his face into the driver and passenger seats.

He looked back at Wow and yelled "Are you still with me!" Wow replied but wasn't audible. During the thought of losing his little cousin, he snatched the seat from the frame of the car. His eyes glowed at the sight of Bunch's AK-47 in front of him. "Thank you lord," Marion said silently.

He grabbed the assault rifle and exited the bullet riddled Chevy. Wow eyes were glazed over as he tried to maintain consciousness. Marion positioned himself along the rear quarter panel. The shooters where surprised when he appeared from behind the car.

"What the fuck," yelled one of the shooters. They were caught off guard from Marion's return fire. The guy with the gold teeth body jerked and shuddered when the .223 caliber slugs plowed into his chest and abdomen. He collapsed to the pavement; his cohort looked at his friend lying on the ground and tried to flee.

The burst from the AK-47 echoed throughout the plaza. Marion shot directly for the dread headed shooter legs. His body buckled under the damage to his limbs. Marion moved from around their car closer to the man with the gold teeth.

The man's breathes was short and shallow. Marion stared him in the eyes pointing the barrel in the man's face. The man cringed sensing his death was imminent. However, Marion decided not to put him out his misery but let him bleed out slowly.

He kicked the man's handgun away carefully walking towards the dread headed shooter. He was crawling along the ground. Marion fire one calculated shot into the dread headed shooter. The high caliber round pierced his cranium and sent skull fragments, brain matter and sinew everywhere.

During the chaos, the driver had backed out and positioned the vehicle facing his deceased comrade. Marion was face to face with the headlights as the SUV sped toward him. He jumped out of the way dodging a puddle of brain matter and dreaded hair in the process.

The driver had no regard; he drove over his friend's mutilated body. It rolled, crackled and squashed under the weight of the speeding vehicle. Marion emptied the clip into the driver side of the vehicle as he sped from the scene.

He quickly ran to the bullet riddled car and checked on Wow. He was barely conscious. Some people came to help. They swerved up in a brown minivan and a gray pickup truck.

"Hey can y'all take Wow to the hospital! He needs a doctor quick," Marion exclaimed to the older guy driving the gray pickup.

"Hell yeah! We can take him," said the driver frantically.

People scooped Wow Wow from the ground and placed him in the bed of the gray pick up. The people held towels against his wounds to slow the bleeding. The pickup sped out the lot; Marion jumped in the minivan and raced to the apartments. He arrived at the apartment's entrance in no time.

Marion felt light headed as he ran to Bunch's house. He forgot about the lacerations on his head and neck. The faster he ran the more the sweat and blood stung. The Woodland residents stood outside staring as the illumination of the police sirens approached the complex.

This was a regular occurrence. The sounds of numerous sirens didn't intimidate anyone; this was a daily thing every summer. The house went hysterical when Marion barged through the back door waving Bunch's AK-47.

People immediately swarmed him asking all types of questions as he tried to catch his breath. Someone turned the radio down so they could hear him speak. He flinched as someone wiped a towel across his cuts.

There was about 20-30 people in the little apartment. Most of the people in the house where ready to go pop some shit off. Wow's baby momma was in tears; yet, Bunch was oddly calm. The entire house and complex knew what happened.

Bunch asked one simple question "Who did it?"

>"It was homeboys of that nigga Peezy he murdered. One of the nigga wore a fitted hat with the MVB initials," Marion told him seeing the pain in his eyes.

>"Nigga....he's all I have! Fuck this house; fuck these bitches. Fuck all this shit," he growled in pain beating on his chest.

Marion felt horrible for having to leave Bunch in his time of need. Everyone knew that if he didn't leave now CPD would lock down the apartments. They would bring out the dogs and the task force; Marion did not need that type of trouble.

He wiped the blood from his head and neck off then looked in the mirror. There was blood on his shirt and shorts. Also there were little blobs of pinkish matter on his shoes which could only be the dread headed guy's brain matter. Bunch quickly gave him a change of clothes and disposed of the bloody ones.

Marion got into his black SUV and drove slowly to the entrance. The police had the apartment lockdown with a single checkpoint to get in and out of the complex. Marion saw that they were checking driver's licenses and searching vehicles. He saw a few get arrested for possession of marijuana.

Marion rolled to the checkpoint feeling nervous. An officer approached the passenger side of the SUV trying to look into vehicle. Yet, Marion's reflective dark tint obscured his view. The other treated the situation as a routine traffic stop.

After 7 minutes of badgering, they let him out of the convoy of police, swat and task enforcement vehicles. Marion sighed in relief as his next destination was his hotel room.

Chapter 2-7

It was 9:22pm when Liyah pulled into Kim's driveway. Her anxiety had her hands clammy and shaking. The thought of explaining her affair had her stomach churning. She noticed Jay's car was gone.

Kim stood in the threshold of their doorway. Liyah walked up to Kim and gave her a hug. The ambience of their house was comforting and inviting. Liyah sat her purse down on table by the door and followed Kim into the kitchen.

Her kitchen was humungous. It was equipped with a breakfast nook, onyx black countertop island and a six-person wet bar with booth. They sat in the corner booth as smooth jazz played over the surround sound. Liyah felt somewhat relieved to express how she felt with someone.

> "Ok. Have you ever wanted to be little kinky in the bedroom," Liyah said.

> "Yeah, I believe we all want to try something new," Kim replied.

> "Well, if you remember the Annual City Council Luncheon that's when it all started," Liyah said which captured Kim's attention.

The banquet hall was brimming with people. The live band played as people conversed with one another. Everyone was assigned a lapel to identify their association. There was a variety of colors signaling the importance of the figures in attendance.

Liyah commented Marion on how dapper he looked in his Brook Brothers suit. She scanned the room and noticed her entourage: Jay, Kim and Mya. She was stunned to see Dave had come along to support her efforts. They all saw her and Marion and rushed over.

They politely congratulated her while Jay ushered the men away quietly. The women snickered amongst each other about their dresses, hair and shoes. The bartender was attracted to four months pregnant Kim; he kept trying to join in the conversation. The room suddenly began to cheer and applaud.

Mya and Kim turned to see what the commotion was about as Liyah glared. She knew all too well who entered the room, Nathan Strokes. He was labeled the city's best attorney. There wasn't a form of law he didn't practice.

With a 97% success rate on cases, his services were in high demand. He strolled through the drones of suits and gowns over to Liyah with a cocky brash expression. She smiled as the room focused on the two best attorneys' in Cleveland converse. She introduced Mya and Kim to Nathan of William & Taylor law firm.

Their conversation was brief. The host for the night took the stage and asked everyone to take their seats. They all sat at their assigned tables. Liyah looked over at William & Taylor's table.

Nate caught Liyah's eyes and smirked. The awards were handed out in 20 minutes. Shortly after the awards there was an intermission. Everyone began to socialize. Nate admired Liyah from the distance as she stood by the bar.

> "You're a really good attorney Ms. Morris. I follow your Cleveland-4 case thoroughly," Nate said sipping his wine.

"Really, that was definitely a monumental case in my career," Liyah said blushing.

They talked personally throughout the night. Suddenly, Liyah felt as if Nate was flirting. She found him attractive but was compelled to dismiss the thought. Marion was her love and her life.

"So Nate where is your wife," Liyah said ignoring her temptations.

"Ha ha ha...I'm single unfortunately. I'm waiting for a woman worth my time," Nate said gazing at Liyah intimately.

She could tell by his eyes that he was admiring her body. However, she wasn't offended because she caught herself doing the same thing. She stared at his dick print in his slacks. It appeared to her that he was packing.

"So what are you plans after this," Nate calmly asked.

"I'm just going to relax that's all," she said.

There was silence between them. Liyah felt bad for wanting to cheat but she hadn't had sex in weeks. The thought of sneaking out aroused her. They stared at each other than exchanged numbers. "I'll text you later, he said before walking off.

Kim's expression was of disbelief. Liyah went to the bathroom to get a breather. She feared that Kim was going to tell Marion. Kim sighed before gathering her words carefully.

"Liyah I can't blame you because you have to think about your needs first. However, you're cheating on Marion. You know he's love you beyond his own life," Kim said with tears forming in her eyes.

"I can't blame you for doing what felt right to you. We all have secrets. Mines are no different than yours. Jay and I been trying to have a baby for over two years. The doctor told me that he's 90% of his sperm is sterile. I wanted our child so bad that I slept with his twin brother," Kim said crying.

Liyah was surprised at that revelation. The thought of Kim being pregnant by Jay's brother had her head spinning. Then it hit her, Jay and his brother shares the same DNA. So the child will biologically be Kim's and Jay's.

It was getting late and she still had to work on her case load. She promised Kim an oath of silence before walking to her car. The summer night heat was dry but there was a slight breeze. When she was close to her exit, Marion texted her *"What you doing, I'll be home shortly."* She replied "I'm on my home. See you when you get home."

Chapter 2-8

Marion drove with his senses wired. Every police car he saw had him on the edge. The streets of downtown Cleveland bustled with people this summer night. "It seemed as if everyone was downtown tonight," Marion thought.

He saw the huge Marriott sign and quickly pulled into the illuminated parking garage. He raced up to his room as his thoughts wandered. Once he entered his room, the visions of the bullets whizzing past his head is all he saw when he closed his eyes. He reeked from the stench of gun powder.

It smelled worse than the day after the Fourth of July. He just wanted to rest. His body was tired; yet, his mind was restless. He lay silently on the bed, until he drifted to sleep.

The slumber was interrupted when his phone rung. He turned over and looked at the alarm clock. "It read 11:45pm. Damn...a nigga can't get any rest," he thought in feeling agitated in the dark and cold room.

He had missed calls, voicemails and texts. He checked the voicemails first and they all summed up the same conclusion. Wow was in terrible condition. The last message from Bunch stated Wow lost a lot of blood and suffered internal hemorrhaging.

The bitter thought of losing his little cousin brought tears to Marion's eyes. He saw Dave had called multiple times. "It was unlike him to call this many times," Marion pondered. He finished checking his notifications as he walked to the bathroom.

He stood in front of mirror and stared at himself. There were aches starting to course through his body. His ribs, chest and abdomen were throbbing. He took off his shirt and immediately saw why his upper body was sore.

He counted seven holes in the front of his bulletproof vest. He took it off and saw three more holes on the back. "Thank you lord," he whispered silently while his fingers ran along the holes.

Marion texted Liyah and she replied "I'm on my home. See you when you get home." He sat his phone down and stared at the big bruises across his chest and side. When he lifted his arms sharp pains coursed down his spine. He immediately took some 800 mg painkillers.

The silence of the room was broken when his phone rang.

    "Dave, Dave, Dave," the phone flashed and vibrated.

    "Hello," Marion said fighting the pain.

    "So the old you is back," Dave said calmly.

    "What are you talking about nigga," Marion said confused in thought.

    "Nigga! You haven't seen the news. Turn on your TV," Dave replied as Marion turned on the TV.

To his surprise, every local channel was airing a story about the shootout. Every station showed the grainy footage of him shooting the assault rifle. He held his head listening to Dave on the phone. He hoped that no one else recognized him.

    "Nigga you know I can spot your ass mile away. So don't be surprised? Anyways, what the fuck happened," Dave said raising his voice.

"It was some MVB niggas that fucked with some nigga named Peezy. Remember, Wow got caught up in his murder a few years back. He just came home today from that shit. They dropped the murder to manslaughter and he took the plea," said Marion flicking through the news channels looking at the story.

"That's fucked up! Well I'll reach out to my connect and get their info. Then we'll know if they are really MVB's. If they are we definitely need to visit Quintana. You know he's a MVB general," Dave said calmly.

"Alright nigga. Get on top of that while I get some rest. I'm sore than a bitch," Marion spat as Dave ended the call.

Marion laid there thinking of his lil cousin. The news withheld the shooters identity and focused on Marion. The shootout happened less than two hours ago; they had already offered a ten thousand dollar bounty for any information.

Marion was mentally exasperated from the night before with Dave and now this situation. Marion usually didn't drink but tonight was an exception. He ordered a bottle of gin and a 2-liter sprite.

This wasn't the answer but he knew it would calm his nerves. Room serviced arrived swiftly. He quickly mixed his concoction into a lemon lime cocktail. He nibbled on the cold pizza as the alcohol soothed his nerves fell back to sleep.

Hours later, Marion awoke in darkness and felt homesick and horny. It could've been from the liquor or the fact they hadn't had sex in four days. Temptation won the battle. He packed his things with one thing in mind "I want to be with my baby." In 10 minutes, he was checked out and heading toward the highway.

Chapter 2-9

Liyah pulled into her driveway and noticed Nate's Escalade. There was someone sitting in the passenger side of his truck. Nate stepped out and leaned against the truck arrogantly with his arms folded. "It's too damn late for your shit," she said as he posed next to his truck.

"What the hell are you doing here Nate? I didn't ask you to come over," Liyah said.

"I asked you earlier if I could see you tonight. Also, I figured I'll surprise you tonight," Nate said.

"What the hell are you talking about…surprise," she said checking the time on her cell phone.

"Remember when you told me your fantasy. You said you wanted to fuck me while I fuck another guy. So I lined that up for us," he said pointing to the passenger side of his truck.

"Oh my god! Not tonight, I'm not in the mood. I have so much on my mind," she said calmly trying not to reject Nate.

Nate grabbed her wrists and hugged her aggressively. "You're not listening to me! Why you acting like this," he said wrapping his arms around her. He leaned in for a kiss but was denied. Liyah pulled away and released herself from his grasp.

"So now you're mad! You don't want me to touch you now? Save that sensitive shit for him! You love this dick," Nate yelled.

"Nigga! Who the hell you yelling at? Also keep your voice down, before you wake my neighbors," Liyah spat feeling her frustration building.

"Hey sorry to interrupt y'all love quarrel. I just want to know are we fucking tonight or what? Cuz if not I can go do something or someone else," said a feminine voice sarcastically stepping out of the truck.

Nate saw the irritated expression in her face. When he released her from his bear hug, her hand went across the side of his face. It was clear to her the other person was a transsexual. The transsexual saw what happened and calmly sat back in the truck. Suddenly, a spotlight was beaming at them from a white car they couldn't identify.

After the light dimmed, the Crown Victoria parked in front of the Nate's truck. A white mid-built security guard stepped out in a black outfit with a yellow with black badge. Liyah recognized him; he was the new nightshift security guard.

"So is everything alright Madam," the security guard asked.

"Yes sir, he was just leaving," Liyah said looking spitefully at Nate.

"I was just leaving," Nate said bitterly getting into his truck.

Nate threw the truck in drive and screeched off. They watched the Escalade leave then the security guard got in his car and left. Liyah gathered her things then walked into the house. Her phone chimed but she ignored the phone. Her focus was getting comfortable.

Just as she was about to get in the shower her phone went chimed again. It was a text from Marion. "I fucking miss you. Also I'm coming home," the message read. She sat the phone down and got in the shower.

The warm water hit her body made her reflect. The thought of Nate grabbing her so aggressively made her shutter. The ligatures on her wrists were sore. She shook the thought off and finished her shower.

Chapter 3-1

When Marion arrived home, he noticed various lights on in the house. "It's after 2:30 in the morning. What she still doing up," he thought. He parked on the street because he knew he was drunk. He stumbled from the vehicle to the front door. He quickly opened the door. Immediately, the rush of cool air made him nauseated.

He leaned over the bannister and vomited in the grass. Liyah heard him hurling and stood in the threshold observing. "You're going to clean that up in the morning," she mumbled. The aroma following him made her stomach queasy. He reeked of alcohol and sulfur.

She maintained her composure but her attention and curiosity was drawn to his bright colored outfit. Since she'd known him, he never wore colors brighter than yellow. Marion stumbled when he noticed her in the doorway.

> "What you still doing up," Marion slurred as Liyah held her nose.
>
> "Ooh! How much have you had to drink? I'm coming from Kim's. We had a long overdue girl talk," Liyah said fanning away the odor.

She guided him into the house and to the bedroom. Even though he was drunk she was happy to see him. She helped him undress and noticed he had scratches and abrasions on his head.

> "The cuts looked like he had been fighting," she thought to herself.

She didn't want to consider cheating but how could he explain the change of clothes. She was about to ask him when Marion interrupted. "What the hell did you do to your arms," he said looking down at her arms. She didn't notice that she had red marks along her wrists and forearms.

The moment when Nate grabbed her flashed vividly. She shrugged off the thought and quickly told him an excuse. His half opened bloodshot eyes roamed up and down body. He slid his hands under her shirt and played with her nipples.

Her excitement aroused him. His dick rose through the opening of his boxers. She did not want him asking any more questions. So she leaned him back on the bed and took off his boxers.

He relaxed as his dick pulsated in her mouth. She loved the way him and Deep Stroke where complete opposites sexually. Deep Stroke's open minded, aggressive, verbal style rivaled Marion's closed minded, passive and charming ways.

Her phone kept chiming and vibrating on the nightstand. "Who the hell is this," he slurred with agitation in his voice. Liyah knew it Deep Stroke arrogant selfish ass. She grabbed the phone from his hand while taking his dick down her throat.

He pumped a few times and she felt him release. Her mouth filled quickly with semen. She hurried to swallow but he kept cumming. After swallowing his third load, he motioned her to get in the bed.

She inserted his dick while straddling him. The slow movements of her hips made his dick throb. A few slow

coordinated strokes brought Marion to a climax. He held her tightly as he licked her titty.
"I'm ready for us to have a baby," he said.

She couldn't believe what he just said. Her thoughts where racing while she cleaned up. "Come get back in bed," he asked. She politely declined. Marion laid there in a daze as his dick got soft.

She checked her phone and had 5 new texts. The first message gave her the location and room number. The remaining messages were short videos of Deep Stroke sucking, fucking and getting fucked.

The sight was enough to make her want to rush out the door. However, there was a big problem...Marion. She knew he came home early because he missed her. Yet, the thought of Deep Stroke's tantalizing sexcapades won the battle.

Marion laid there with his eyes barely open rubbing his chest. "He's about to go to sleep," she thought. She threw on some sweats and put her hair back into a ponytail. Marion stirred to life mumbling something.

> "What you doing? Come get in bed," he slurred in a raspy voice.
>
> "Honey I can't...Marsha going through some things at home. I promise I won't be too long babe," she said lying putting on her bra.

He agreed as he closed his eyes and began snoring slightly. She gathered her belongings and scurried to her car. She was out the driveway and on the highway within minutes. *"A part of her knew that this was wrong.*

If Marion would've done this to her she'd be furious. The words Kim said earlier echoed to her conscious "Marion's a good man! He treats you damn good!" However, that is true but the department that matters to her he's not that damn good" she thought as she drove to Hilton Garden.

She arrived at the hotel and her heart was racing. Every time they would be together intimately he always took her higher than the time before. She took the elevator to his floor. It traveled so quickly that she didn't even get to finish her text telling him she was at the hotel.

She walked down the hallway looking for room 1048. There was an anxiety building. She always wanted to experience this fantasy; however, she wasn't sure what to expect. He had the executive suite at the end of the hallway. It was distinguished brown door with metallic trim.

She stood before the door trying to collect her thoughts. Her considerate side wanted to be home with her man; yet her selfish side wanted to stay and play. There was a loud "thud" against the door that startled her. There were slight sounds of moaning that dissipated.

Her panties were moistened from the anticipation. She punched in the room code as the mechanism unlocked the door. The room was dimly lit and cold. The aroma of the burning candles gave the room an intimate ambiance.

She closed the door softly. Her eyes focused on the huge bed. Deep Stroke was lying down masturbating while the transsexual licked his feet. Liyah felt an intense euphoric high.

Everything was a blur to Liyah from the oral to the anal sex. The other guy ate her pussy and pinched her nipples while

Deep Stroke pounded her into submission. They slowly untangled their bodies after their orgasms. Liyah laid there collecting her thoughts. This was the best sex she'd ever experienced.

While she was lying there, reality hit her like a ton of bricks. Deep Stroke didn't pull out when he climaxed. She leaned over and rubbed his chest as the other guy sucked his dick. He was enjoying the attention from both of them.

"Baby did you cum," she said softly.

"You know I did. I've wanted to fuck you so bad! Busted all up in there...that's my pussy now," he said arrogantly rubbing her ass.

"What the fuck you mean! Why in the hell would you do that," she yelled looking at him in disgust.

She was furious that he would do such a thing. One thing was on her mind, "Go Home!" Deep Stroke and the transsexual watched her get dressed and stormed out the room. Kim's voice kept reciting in her psych "Marion's a good man! He treats you damn good!" The ride home was harsh. Deep Stroke called at least 17 times. At this point, there was nothing she could do.

She sat in her car and looked up the number to the women's clinic in Fairview Hospital. The clinic's automated machine set her an appointment anytime during business hours tomorrow. She knew Cleveland had one of the most advanced prenatal organizations in the country. A few years ago, she had a one night stand and with a guy who came in her. The clinic was about to tell her the next day she was pregnant.

When she got home, she quietly crept to the bedroom. Marion was sound asleep the way she left him. "Girl why would you treat a man this good so wrong," she thought but didn't have an answer. She slid in next to him and snuggled under his arm. The comfort of being with soothed her enough to go to sleep.

Chapter 3-2

Liyah awoke from the warmth of the sun on her face. The aroma of fresh bacon filled the air. Her alarm clock read 10:37am. She got up and walked downstairs to the kitchen. Marion was cooking breakfast. She sat on a stool and admired him.

"Look at my man. He is so strong and loving. Why would you do this to him? I should tell him about Nate. Uggh last night, I don't know what the fuck Nate was thinking," she thought.

Marion uttered her name while she stared off in space. He ignored her expression. He sat her plate on the table. His focus was on visiting Wow Wow after that horrendous night.

"Liyah…how was your day yesterday," Marion said sarcastically.

"It was alright honey. If you haven't heard my client committed suicide. Then Kim wanted to have a girls night out," she said in rubbing her temples.

"I'm sorry to hear that you went through that babe. My night was cool until a fight broke out over my cousin's house," Marion said lying.

"Okay because I saw the cuts and wounds on your head. I wondered what the hell happened," she said.

Marion was hung over and his body was sore. Yet, Liyah gave awkward glances at the bruises as if fathoming his lie. He disregarded her looks while making their plates

He gave Liyah her plate as they sat at the breakfast table. She turned on the TV and they were talking about gang influences on the city.

> *"I have a report from the Cleveland Police Dept. stating 15 known gangs are operating throughout the city. They have already busted and arrested numerous gang leaders and affiliates. The number one gang they're after goes by the initials MVB which stands for Murder Ville Bloods. They've been linked to murders, extortion, racketeering and plethora of illicit activities.*
>
> *The last gang which had this much impact on the city was the QMB. State and Federal agents worked together to bring down this syndicate that terrorized the 90's. Federal lawyer Nathan Strokes along with his colleagues dismembered the organization and made sure key people would spend a longtime in prison,"* said the TV news reporter.

They both watched the report intently but for different reasons. Marion was taken aback from what he just heard. "Damn! Jay was right, that lawyer Nathan Strokes fucked everything up," he thought. "If I ever run into that Nathan Strokes nigga they'll never have to worry about him again," Marion said in frustration.

Liyah was shocked at Marion's outburst. Now the pressure to keep Nate and Marion separate intensified. She knew Nate but he never stated he worked that high profile case. She read the case file and all the attorney and informant names were blacked out. Liyah's phone vibrated with a text alert from the women's clinic stating she could come in today.

"So how was your night," Liyah asked.

"Well, nothing really out of the ordinary. Me and Dave met up and handled business. The usual shit babe," Marion said.

Liyah knew he was lying but didn't want to press the issue. They continued to eat when Marion's phone rang. He went into the living room and grabbed his phone. Marion saw he had a missed call from Dave. He texted a reply and finished his breakfast.

"So I take it you're about to leave," she demanded.

"Liyah! Really stop acting brand new and shit," Marion replied putting his plate in the sink.

"Nigga don't give me that shit! You just got home and we haven't spent any time together! Now you're leaving out again! I haven't seen you in two days! That's bullshit," she yelled with anger in her voice.

"Liyah, don't fucking start! Please don't," Marion pleaded as he went upstairs and got dressed.

"Fuck that shit, you're fucking wrong," she yelled.

"Well since we're talking about right and wrong. Where the fuck did you go last night? I wasn't that damn drunk," he stated.

His statement caught her off guard. She wasn't expecting his to remember. A pause crept in the back of her throat as doubt slipped in her mind. "Does he know…and he's not saying anything," she thought.

Marion broke her concentration by laughing. "Just know if you are seeing some nigga. I hope he's worth it. If any nigga come to my door with that bullshit its curtains for you and him," he said. She ignored his threat and waved her hand in dismissal. Yet, deep inside herself she knew he meant every word.

Marion trotted downstairs and sat in the living room. It was apparent he was waiting on a ride. She left well enough alone and didn't speak upon it anymore. "Well if you're coming back anytime soon, let me know Marion," she said waltzing into the kitchen with and attitude. "Alright," he said.

Chapter 3-3

Marion hated walking out on Liyah but it kept him from cursing her out. His mind began to wonder. "She wouldn't cheat on me," he thought chuckling to himself. However, her actions last night made him question her loyalty.

"She's usually never up after 2 am. Then she had nerves to leave back out after she just got in the house. We're going to have a nice little talk," he thought briefly before switching his emotions back to business.

His phone chimed and he was in motion. He knew it was Dave because he blew his horn twice when he arrived. Marion brushed off the thoughts he had towards Liyah. He grabbed his fitted hat and headed for the door.

Dave was driving a burgundy tinted Nissan Maxima. It was already understood why he had the car. Today, Quintana was going to meet his maker. They exited the driveway and headed for the south side.

They arrived at Quinlan's Auto Body shop. The company belonged to Quintana's father until his death. Now the shop was a front for Quintana's dealings. He dealt with everything from money laundering to chopping cars.

They walked into the building about 11:20am. They asked to speak with the owner; however, the receptionist declined. Dave whispered something in her ear. She smiled and pointed to the offices in the back.

They walked through the glass door. The shop floor was busy with mechanics working on customers vehicles. The radio was barely audible from the loud "whirring" of the pneumatic air tools. The whole garage smelled like a concoction of motor oil, gasoline and diesel fuel.

Immediately, a vehicle at the back of the shop caught Marion's attention. It was a 90's model GMC Yukon that had been stripped and primed. The doors, fenders and hood were missing. Also, it appeared that someone was in the process of taking out the interior.

Marion and Dave decided to take a closer look. There were several bullet holes throughout the body of the vehicle. It was very obvious to Marion that this was the truck the shooters had last night. The rear hatch was still attached and hadn't been primed.

Marion's anger churned but Dave did his best to keep him calm. They walked towards the dirty hallway that displayed a timeline of photos of the shop owner. There were smudges and oil stains on the floor and walls. At the end of the hallway was a door that read "main office." Dave knocked and a voice replied "enter."

They entered the air conditioned office and the aroma of potent marijuana filled the air. There were two men sitting on a couch and another behind the office desk. The men glared at Marion with a distasteful stare. However, it appeared that Dave knew the men.

"Daveno! So nice of you to visit. What brings you this way," said the rotund man behind the desk.

"What's up Action! I came down here to talk with Q," Dave said after introducing Marion. They spoke briefly before Action dismissed one of the men on the couch.

The other guy left on the couch was Chevy and the man behind the desk was Action. Their reputation of extortion and violence was infamous. Marion recalled Dave telling him they were Quintana's top henchmen. They looked very treacherous and conniving.

Chevy finished rolling his blunts. He pulled a saucer plate of cocaine from underneath the coffee table. It was obvious he was high and drunk. Chevy offered him a seat but Marion declined.

Dave told Action the situation about Wow. Everything was alright until Chevy started running his mouth. Action told him to shut up and he obliged. Action agreed to look into what happened and speak to Quintana about it.

Yet, Chevy couldn't control himself.

>"Look my nigga! That's fucked up that your man's got hit. However, he crossed the MVB and we don't let nothing slide," he said while snorting a line off the plate.

>"Nigga watch your mouth," Marion said sternly.

>"Naah, if you really want to know. We been had it in for that nigga. I'm surprised he lasted this long. My niggas was at his throat soon as he got in his cell," Chevy said spitefully.

So fuck what he talking. I'm glad the nigga got hit. If I had it my way I would've killed him myself," he said chugging the last of his of Hennessy with coke on his nose.

Marion lost control and punched Chevy in his mouth. His lips exploded with blood gushing from his mouth. The initial punch stunned him causing him to drop his saucer of coke. Chevy threw a couple punches to defend himself to no avail.

His punches didn't faze Marion. He kept swinging with each punch making a loud "thud" sound. Chevy tried to protect his head but Marion's punches where powerful. The fifth or sixth blow to his head rendered him unconscious.

Each blow jerked his head back violently. His eyes had swelled shut as blood spewed from his nose. Marion was relentless in his assault. "Bitch ass nigga! I told you to watch your motherfucking mouth," he exclaimed while pounding his fist into his skull.

Action recognized Chevy was in bad shape and needed help. He tried to reach for his pistol but was deterred.

>"You don't need to be touching that," Dave said sarcastically laying his .40cal Sig Sauer on the desk.

Action yelled "Get your motherfucking nigga! He's going to kill him!" Dave pointed his gun at Action and demanded "Keep your hands where I can see them." Action complied as Dave stopped Marion. Chevy's face was battered, bloodied and swollen.

Dave pushed Marion out the door while keeping his gun pointed at Action. Marion was furious. However, Dave shouted "He had enough! Let's fucking go!" Marion complied.

They quickly got into their car. Marion explained why he beat Chevy's ass in the office. Dave understood but was concerned that would pit them against the MVB.

"Fuck the MVB! They can get it like anybody else, they're not invincible," Marion exclaimed.

"You right, fuck'em. Anyways, you riding with me to the hospital or you going solo," Dave said.

"Liyah wants to go with me. So just drop me off at home and we'll meet y'all up there," Marion said.

Chapter 3-4

Marion strolled into the house and immediately felt sadness. He didn't want to see Wow Wow clinging to life on a hospital bed. The house was filled with the sounds of Liyah's music. The sound system had the condo shaking.

Whenever, she blasted her music she was usually pissed off about something. *"Fuck it, she'll be alright. I don't have time for her shit today,"* Marion thought going upstairs. He entered the bedroom and plopped down on the bed. He grabbed the remote and turned down her music.

She peeked around the corner "you didn't have to turn it down that low. Also are we still going to the hospital," she said. Marion nodded as he lay back on the bed resting his eyes. It was obvious he was tired. At times she wished he would just understand her more.

Liyah walked in and sat down a basket of laundry. Immediately, she noticed that she forgot to close her night stand drawer. It was half open with her strap-on partially sticking out. She sat on the bed and made small talk with Marion while sliding the drawer closed with her leg.

"Good thing he isn't the noisy," she thought momentarily. "Well I'm about to get dressed now. Babe I have an appointment to be at after we leave. Do you know how long we're going to be up there," Liyah said getting off the bed grabbing some clothes from the laundry basket.

> "I don't know but I don't plan to be up there that long. You know how I feel about hospitals," he sighed.

She quickly dressed and they headed downstairs. Liyah opted to drive. She dropped the top as Marion reclined his seat. The sun beamed as they headed for the hospital.

When they arrived at Fairview Hospital there wasn't anywhere to park on ground level. "Damn it's nowhere to park," Marion said. "Babe it's 12:30pm what'd you expect at lunchtime. Also you can go in and I'll park the car. Just call me and tell me where y'all going to be at," she said. Liyah pulled up to the main entrance and Marion got out. He disappeared inside while Liyah drove to the parking garage.

She called the woman's clinic advising them she will be signing in shortly. She found a parking spot on the 9th level as her phone vibrated. "We are on the 7th floor, East wing room 728," read the message from Marion. "SO YOU GOT A FUCKING ATTITUDE. WHAT YOU EXPECT…YOU KNOW YOU GOT SOME GOOD PUSSY. YOU CAN'T SAY I DIDN'T EARN IT," read Nate's text. She ignored his message and got out the car.

Liyah crossed the skywalk into the main building. She went to the central atrium and caught the elevator to the 7th floor West wing. When she arrived at Wow Wow's room it was spacious and calm. He was hooked up to various machines with wires running everywhere.

Mya and Dave sat in the corner on a dark brown couch. Marion was standing by a window talking to his cousin Bunch. Mya saw Liyah and quietly got up and gave her a hug. "Jay and Kim is here as well they stepped out for a moment," Mya said.

The door opened and Jay and Kim entered followed by Wow Wow's doctors. The room fell silent at the sight of the doctors while the sounds of the medical machines continued to beep.

"Hello I'm Dr. Stokowski and this is my assistant Dr. Chancellor. We're going to be Mr. Barter's surgical team. Mr. Barter suffered internal damage to his left lung, 7th and 8th vertebrae and hemorrhaging of his kidney. We've stabilized his vital but more surgery will be required," said the doctor.

Liyah tapped Marion on the shoulder "Babe I'll be right back," she said. Marion agreed barely hearing her words. She walked back to the elevator and went down to the 5th floor. The elevator was swift.

When she got off the elevator, she noticed a lot of things changed since the last time she had been there. The entire floor now belonged to the Women's Health Clinic. She walked through the automatic sliding glass doors. "How may I help you today," said the receptionist. "I'm here for an appointment," Liyah told her.

She signed in and waited briefly for her name to be called. The office was empty as she took a seat. A nurse called her instantaneously. "Morris, may you come back now," said the doctor.

Dr. Wheeling was polite as she gathered specimens. Liyah was in and out of her office within 35 minutes. They told her the complete results would be available in three days. She went back upstairs to the 9th floor hoping Marion didn't notice her hiatus.

When she got off the elevator, she was met by Kim and Mya standing in the lobby. "Where have you been girl," they said. "I had to take a business call. Where is everyone," she asked.

Mi'Shele: Da Streets are Callin Me Pt. 1   page| 102

Kim informed her that Wow had just gone into surgery. "Also Dave, Jay, Bunch and Marion are in the room talking business," Mya said.

Marion burst out the room in frustration followed by Dave. "Babe may you take me home, now," demanded Marion. Liyah obliged knowing he must have heard some bad news. Usually, if Marion was upset about something so was Dave. Jay walked out the room and hugged Kim. "Thanks for the support y'all; I'm a stay up here with him," said Bunch.

They all got on the elevator and went up to the 9th floor. Once they crossed the sky bridge they all separated and located their cars. Marion hadn't said a word to Liyah. During the whole home, he was quiet and in a cogitative state.

When they arrived home, Liyah kissed him passionately once they got in the house. She could tell he was hurting over the situation with Wow. She embraced him tightly then he excused himself to make a phone call.

The phone call was brief. He had an agitated expression on his face while sitting in the living room. Liyah went in the other room and texted Nate. "Honk, honk" was the sound they heard from outside. "I out of here babe," Marion said as he left out the door.

Chapter 3-5

Marion was home no longer than 10 minutes before Dave pulled up in a burgundy Nissan Maxima. The sun was still high in the afternoon. They stopped at Bella's Bar & Grill. Marion knew the owner for years. He was a mid-class gun runner with a decent arsenal of weapons. Marion was in and out within 15 minutes.

He walked back to the car with a large black draw string bag. Dave grabbed the bag when Marion got into the car. They drove to the far side of town hoping Action or Chevy didn't tip off Quintana. That would ruin their plans.

Dave guided Marion to one of Quintana's stash spots on the other side of town. When they pulled up Dave saw Quintana's tangerine colored corvette parked outside. Marion and Dave parked at the corner and waited for him to return to his car. People often stated Quintana looked like an in shape Gucci Mane. He always wore lavish jewelry and drove custom cars; however, he kept a gun on him at all times.

Every street nigga in the city knew his reputation. He's shot niggas, beat two murders and a dope case. However; word throughout the city, he was wanted. It was rumored that some Memphis head cutters had a whole brick on his head.

He emerged from the tri-level building with a duffle bag and two burly men by his side. The men displayed their firearms to warn off any potential robbers or jack boys. Quintana surveyed his surroundings and tossed the duffle into his trunk. The tangerine colored corvette then zoomed out the parking lot. Marion followed him closely in their burgundy Maxima.

Dave sat quietly in the passenger seat with his mask and gun on his lap. He grabbed a silencer from the bag between his feet and bobbed his head to the music. "It was crazy how a week ago, Quintana was one of his best clients; now he wanted to blow his brains out," Marion thought looking at Dave twist the silencer on his Sig Saur. There was no turning back.

> "I can't believe he gave the order! Better yet he knew it was your cousin! That's some snake shit! After all the times we'd threw him extras," Dave ranted in fury.

Action's smug statement resonated within Marion. He figured if he has to plan his cousin's funeral someone's going to be planning Quintana's. The tangerine corvette made two stops. He stopped at Phase Three Pool & Bar and then Woodhill Park.

A young goon wearing a dingy white beater ran to the car as the corvette's truck lifted. He grabbed the duffle bag from Quintana's trunk and trotted over to a triple black Jaguar XJ. He handed the bag to someone in the backseat. The young goon quickly sat back atop one of the numerous candy colored cars.

He talked with other teens as he watched the perimeter. Their entourage had more than twenty plus niggas from Marion's point of view. From their assortment of red and tan colors, he knew they were MVB's.

Quintana parked his corvette amidst various candy colored cars. He talked with the thugs and goons for about 35 minutes. Marion and Dave sat across the lot watching the group. "Hand me the Uzi," Marion said sternly eyes brimming with hate.

Dave reached back into the bag and dug past a sawed-off shotgun, couple handguns and a small AK-47 without a stock. The black fully automatic modified Uzi was at the bottom of the bag. Dave knew Marion meant business when he saw the small 150 round mini drum.

>"Damn...nigga stop running your mouth," Marion blurted in frustration looking at Quintana.

>"Fuck'em! Swing this bitch around and pull up in front of them niggas" Dave replied grabbing the AK-47 and putting the handgun in his waistline.

Marion looked at Dave. One thing he respected about Dave; if business needed to be handled; he'll handle it no matter the situation. The park was packed with people cooking, playing basketball and enjoying the hot afternoon. Marion was eager to ease his pain through the barrel of his Uzi.

He was about to pull from his parking spot when four officers ran past their car. "Freeze! Don't fucking move," yelled an officer as law enforcement descended on the black luxury sedan. People throughout the park scattered from all the commotion. A couple of officers shot at the Jaguar.

"*Screech*," was the sound as the jaguar shot in reverse. Three officers in the car's path couldn't escape the mayhem. The black sedan sped backwards and hit'em hard tossing them into the sky.

People from the entourage opened fire at the approaching officers.

The young goon with the dingy white beater emptied his magazine before getting blown away. The blast from the tactical officer's 12-gauge exploded his chest and abdomen. Within moments, majority of the mislead teens laid lifeless on the ground. The few that returned fire either surrendered shortly after or met their demise.

The jaguar stopped and barrels emerged from behind the dark tinted windows. Bullets flew from the driver and passenger windows as the officers retreated and took cover. They returned fire on the sedan as it sped away. Marion watched the bust unfold as Dave focused on Quintana.

> "What the fuck," Marion yelled putting the car in gear.

> "I don't know but we definitely need to get away from here," Dave said putting the guns and masks in the bag.

Officers swarmed the area dispatching ambulances and transport wagons. Marion and Dave where dumbfounded at what just occurred.

> "Damn! That motherfucker is the luckiest bastard....," Marion ranted before being interrupted by Dave.

> "Slow down a bit. I think that's him walking right there," he said pointing through the tinted window.

They pasted him slowly as they debated on an approach. Marion stopped the car about 20ft ahead of Quintana. Dave leaned out the window and called his name. He was hesitant until he recognized Dave.

He quickly sprinted to the car and got in. Quintana was surprised to see Marion and Dave. He began to explain what happened as they listened intently. "Shit!.....Fuck! I left my phone in the fucking car," he said angrily patting his pockets.

"He hasn't talked with Action or Chevy," Marion thought. Quintana asked if they could take him Quinlan's. Marion felt his anger surging the more Quintana spoke. He cringed when he said "Niggas like us is too real for the streets."

While waiting at a red light, Marion glanced at Dave's pistol. Marion grabbed the gun and spun around. "Pew pew," was the sound of the suppressed gunshots. Quintana's head thumped against the dark tinted window from the force of the shots.

He didn't know what hit him as the bullets pierced the left side of his skull. Blood squirted profusely from a fracture in his head and nose. His body tensed up and slumped against the passenger door. Quintana's bright colored outfit was now crimson red.

Dave jerked around and looked at Marion. His cold, bleak, desolate expression shocked him. The car behind them honked their horn. Marion glanced forward and saw that the light had turned green.

Marion didn't say a word to Dave. When they turned onto 116st, Quintana's tensed body fell on the seat. Dave saw the tip of the slug bulging above his right eyebrow. There was four inch long fracture from the top of his eyebrow to his hairline. Blood oozed from the fracture into his lifeless bloodshot eyes.

Marion called Jay and simply said "pick us up at Gerald's. Also wire him $15,000." They drove to Gerald's Salvage & Junkyard. They pulled into the back and parked next to the owner's green Chrysler 300. They was all too familiar with the process.

Dave went inside; Marion waited in the car. Dave reappeared from the building with Gerald. He was an overweight middle aged ex-construction. Marion stepped out the car as Gerald greeted him with a firm handshake.

They conversed about past times then immediately got to business. Marion stepped aside as Gerald peeked in the car. He shook his head and looked at them questionably. "Really guys! You just couldn't keep it clean? Y'all have to make a mess," he said closing the door.

Gerald got on his walkie-talkie and dispatched for a driver. After their short conversation, a large yellow lift emerged from the machine shop. Gerald flagged the driver out the vehicle. "Hey Donald take a break. I'll cover you," he said to the driver.

Dave grabbed the black draw string bag as Gerald lifted the car in the air. They knew where to go as they walked to the compactor. Marion thought about Wow's funeral arrangements.
He quickly dismissed the thought.

Gerald had a state of the art compactor. It was three stories tall and a mile long. They walked upstairs to the observation deck. They watched Gerald drop the blood stained Maxima into the compactor.

They talked amongst themselves about the bullshit that happened earlier. Gerald entered the air conditioned room and headed over to the controls. "Hey thanks for that payment. My receptionist informed me your payment just posted," he said starting the machine.

The hydraulic pumps groaned and hummed. The car's suspension popped and crackled as the compactor flattened the car. The pressures exerted left the car tall as an end table. Gerald pressed a couple buttons and the ceiling retracted.

The sides compacted squeezing the car to 96x24x24 rectangle. The final phase of the compaction brought the rectangle to 56x24x24. The compactor stopped as Gerald operated the drop claw. He picked up the block of metal and blood and sat it on a conveyor belt.

The metal block traveled into the attached metal refinery. Marion glanced at his phone and saw a text from Jay. "I'm here," read the message. He tapped Dave on the shoulder and nudged his head towards the door.

Marion signaled their departure. Marion and Dave saw Jay's silver S600 parked amongst the cars. Once they got in they told him what transpired throughout their day.

Chapter 3-6

Marion had just relaxed in their spacious living room when the doorbell chimed "ding dong." It was 5pm. He wasn't expecting anyone so he ignored it. On the third chime, he answered the door.

"Who is it," Marion asked.

"Fed Ex," said a stern masculine voice.

He opened the door and saw a huge brown teddy bear and a few dozen roses. Marion was surprised at the sight. "Package for Marion Darby," said the delivery man waiting for his signature. Marion signed for the package and sat the items in the foyer.
There was an envelope laced with Liyah's favorite perfume "Reflections." The envelope contained a pink card with brief poem on it which read.

"Our DEEP love endures more than most, I've devoted my life and heart to you so. We'll be forever bonded STROKE like molasses, passionate as a kiss or nasty with tongue in my ass.

To my world...

It appeared Liyah was trying to be loving and caring but he thought differently. The thought of her cheating was now prominent. The only time she done this was when another guy kissed her years ago.

About 30 minutes later, Liyah came home. She sat her bags down in the kitchen and walked towards the living room. Marion was lounging in a white beater and some boxers. "Hey baby how you doing. Babe put that up," she said after noticing the head of his dick showing through his boxers.

Her attention shifted when she saw the huge teddy bear. Before she could speak, Marion held up the pink card teasingly. "So you missed me, huh? So...you want to get your ass licked," he said stroking his hard dick with his free hand. Liyah suppressed her confused expression.

She went along with Marion's ranting's. She yanked the card from his fingers. Marion words sounded distant as she read the poem on the card. Her temper immediately boiled.

> *"Now Nate is out of fucking control! I'm bout to cuss this motherfucker out! Uggh...why in the hell would he send this to Marion,"* she thought concealing her aggression.

Marion grabbed her hips and pulled her close. He could see the silhouette of her hardening nipples through her blouse. "Take your ass upstairs," Marion said intimately caressing her thighs. Liyah relished in the attention and rushed upstairs.

Her mind pondered Nate's intentions behind the deliver. She quickly removed her clothes and lay across the bed. "He's been acting very spiteful lately. He just shows up at my house unannounced, arguing and now this shit. I'm done dealing with this shit," she thought.

Marion quickly flipped her onto her stomach. At that moment, she knew they were going to be a while. Marion dozed off after beating the pussy relentlessly. When he awoke he saw Liyah standing in the bathroom. She appeared frustrated holding her phone tightly staring in the mirror. "Let's just get this over with damn," she exclaimed before storming into the bedroom.

She sat on the bed and stared into space with a cogitative expression. Marion felt a surge of dislike in his gut. He remained motionless watching her through his squinted eyes. Marion lay silently questioning his relationship and Liyah's loyalty.

He got up like he'd just awoken. "Did you sleep well," she said when she rubbed his back. Marion ignored her; Liyah felt the tension and let him be.

> "I'll be back. Kim wants me to come over," he said scrolling through his phone.
>
> "Oh ok babe. I'll be here," Liyah replied nervously.

She wasn't sure what to think. Marion woke up with an attitude and Kim wanted to talk. Liyah took a deep breath because the situation was out of her hands. *"Well if she tell him then it is what it is. I have bigger things to worry about,"* she told herself.

Marion left without a goodbye or a kiss. She knew he was upset about something but she'll figure that out later. "Well I might as well get this meeting over with," she thought sighing as she called Nate. He answered "I'm pulling up now."

Chapter 3-7

When Liyah got into the truck she had to calm her nerves. She was ready to go the fuck off on Nate. "That little stunt he pulled mailing that shit to Marion," was very vivid in her mind. She washed up quickly and put on some leggings and t-shirt. "Let me check one more time to make sure I'm not forgetting anything," she thought before heading out the door.

She got in the Escalade and they drove to Cleveland Clinic Liyah was surprised by how quiet and reserved Nate was today. He hadn't said much since she got in the truck.

> "Well that package you sent was cute. Also I just left my doctor's office," Liyah said sarcastically.
>
> "Hey...a gift from the man you fuck to the man you love. Obviously, the gift worked because you look refreshed. Did he fuck you like I do? Also I don't give a damn about your doctor! I need to know you truly went," he said smirking.
>
> "If me and my man fucked that's none of your damn business. You need to be concerned with this situation," she said as he remained silent.
>
> *"I know he's not bitching up. He was big bad ass a couple nights ago when you came in me. So deal with it,"* she thought.

They pulled into the parking lot and quickly parked. Cleveland Clinic was huge. His doctor was located in the main building on the 20th floor. They got there quick it was only 6:30pm. They waited for the elevator, her phone vibrated. It was a text from Marion but she quickly silenced the alert.

As they reached the 20th floor Nate's phone rang. People chuckled as when they heard Michael Jackson singing "Billy Jean is not my lover." Nate glanced at his phone deciding whether to ignore or answer. Liyah looked at his phone and saw the name Coral TS. "If you want to answer don't let me stop you," she said.

Nate sent the call to voice mail. They exited the elevator and walked into the doctor's office. The office was spacious with a couple of people waiting in the reception area. Liyah signed in and waited for her named to be called.

It was obvious that something was heavily on Nate's mind. He had barely said anything to her since he picked her up. He just kept looking at his phone as if he was expecting a call or message. *"Well if he don't want to talk that's fine,"* she thought wondering if Kim told Marion anything.

Nate's phone rang again. He sighed in annoyance. "Nate what's the matter? You haven't said much of anything today. Are you nervous about me being pregnant," she said. He simply replied "I have much more important thing to consider." Liyah was about to cuss him out when the nurse called her name. Nate reassured her as he answered his phone.

The doctor's small stature shocked Liyah. The Middle Eastern woman stood a bit over 4ft 5in with long black hair like Kim. It was obvious why Nate liked his doctor. She was very attractive with very tone physique.

The woman was very cordial. She collected urine, blood and hair samples. The visit took no longer than 30 minutes. "Ms.

Morris we should have your results within the next hour. You may wait if you want; however, most of our patients prefer us to call them with the results," said the doctor. Liyah agreed to have them call her.

When Liyah walked back into the reception area, Nate was pacing by the window upset. "Who the fuck you think I am bitch," Liyah heard him mumble aggressively into the phone. He ended the call swiftly when he saw Liyah. "Hey babe? Do you want to get something to eat? I'm hungry," he asked calmly when they left the office.

Liyah refused to get in his business and personal affairs. She simply agreed to his offer to get something to eat as they walked to his truck. "Let's go to Chick-Fil-A. I haven't had that in a while," Liyah said.

The restaurant was minutes away from the hospital. When they arrived at Chick-Fil-A, Nate stared at Liyah with a heartbroken expression. She couldn't decide whether to hold him or demand "what's wrong!" Forty minutes had past when he finally gathered his composure and went inside to order.

Liyah checked her phone while she waited in the truck. She got tired of listening to 106.9 FM, they wasn't playing anything good. Liyah knew Nate kept his music cd's in his center console. Her phone rang and she froze with fear. It was the doctor calling with the results.

She was torn between the truth and the lie, lust vs. love and the outcome wasn't going to be pretty. Liyah took a deep breath and answered the phone "Hello." Immediately, she could sense something was wrong from the numerous unrelated questions the doctor began to ask. "Hey...I don't know what's with all the questions but may you get to point," Liyah exclaimed out of frustration.

> *"I can handle the truth! Either I'm pregnant or I'm not," she told herself.*

The doctor continued with her questions ranging from family diseases to diet and exercise. She answered the questions while she continued looking for cd's. Inside the center console was a cluster of papers, cd's and knick knacks. Her attention was suddenly drawn to his cluster of papers.

The letter head of the hospital sparked her curiosity. She knew he was in good health but she continued to read the papers. The test shown his STD and Hiv/Aids test but the results were inconclusive. She knew last month when they got tested he was negative
.
Her mind wondered then the doctor asked if she could return ASAP. Liyah demanded the reason for the urgency. "Ms. Morris I have good news and bad news...the good news is you are pregnant. However, I'm sorry to inform you of the bad because you're obviously unaware. You've tested positive for Hiv," said the doctor.

Liyah was speechless, clueless, confused along with a plethora of other emotions. "Let me call you back," she said bleakly. She stared at Nate's results in disbelief before placing them back in the console. She wept silently to herself.

Nate returned with the food and saw that Liyah was distraught. He decided not to ask what was wrong because she looked furious. He started the truck and they left Chick-Fil-A. She remained silent while glaring out the window.

"Liyah what's the matter! Are you nervous about being pregnant! Say something damn," Nate demanded turning down the radio.

"Nathan I've always been honest with you. Is there anything you need to tell me...now is the motherfucking time, Liyah said sarcastically calm staring at the red traffic light.

"What! Naah I don't," he replied waiting for the light to turn green.

"What the fuck is this," Liyah yelled with tears falling from her eyes reaching for the papers in the console.

Nate eyes widen with a surprised expression. Liyah threw the papers in his face before he could say a word. She unbuckled her seatbelt and started punching, slapping and yelling at him. He tried to focus on the road as the traffic light turned green.
They didn't make completely into the intersection when they heard a loud "screeeeeech" followed by "boom!" They got T-boned on the passenger side by car that was fleeing from the police. Liyah was viciously thrown around the cabin. Her head smashed against the door as her arm snapped.

Nate was knocked unconscious from the impact of the accident. Their truck spun as it crossed the median into oncoming traffic. Motorists weaved and swerved to dodge the mangled Escalade. Just when their truck came to rest, it was hit by a driver that couldn't stop in time.

Liyah's head smacked the ceiling and windshield. There was blood pouring from the top of her head. She felt very disoriented and light headed. "Aggggh, Help me," she whimpered in agony.

There was an intense tingling sensation along the right side of her body. Her vision was blurred from the blood dripping in her eyes. She noticed the dashboard had crumpled against her legs. Just as a policeman rushed to her aid, she passed out from a loss of blood.

Chapter 3-8

During his drive, Marion was unsure why Kim wanted to see him so urgently. He didn't care it gave him a reason to get out of Liyah's presence. Lately, he's been feeling frustrated with her actions. "If you're unhappy bitch then leave," Marion yelled thinking out loud.

When he pulled into Kim's driveway he saw Jay was home. He parked and went into the house. "Hey Marion? We need to talk when you and Kim get done," Jay said looking down onto the entrance from upstairs. Kim was in the kitchen cooking.

Marion walked into the kitchen smelling the wonderful aroma. "Hey Kim how you doing," Marion said kissing her on the cheek. She acknowledged offering him a seat. Marion accepted pouring him something to drink.

> "Marion I know you wondering why I called you to come over here," Kim said rotating her roast.
>
> "Yeah, what's going on? I thought you went into labor or something," Marion said.
>
> "Hey before we get into this what time is it? So I know when this roast is done," Kim said.
>
> "Uggh it's 6:42pm," Marion replied.

Kim chuckled while putting the roast back into the oven. Marion began to wonder what she was about to say. The thoughts and feelings he had toward Liyah reached a pinnacle. He texted Liyah "It's some shit going on that needs to be cleared up. Call me when you get this!"

Kim stirred her simmering vegetables before taking a seat on stool. Marion sensed that this was going to be a heart to heart conversation. He prepared for the worse. Kim took a sip from her cup before speaking.

> "Marion, I love you like a brother. However, it's some things going on I need to tell you. Promise me you won't say nothing or act differently towards what I say," Kim said emotionally.

> "Kim...what the fuck is going on," Marion demanded before being interrupted.

> "Marion can you promise me this...I need to know," Kim pleaded.

> "Yeah...I promise. Now tell me what's going on," Marion said sternly.

Kim sighed heavily and told Marion the truth about her pregnancy. He was shocked but more puzzled why she's telling him now. He felt confused. He wasn't sure who side to take Kim's or Jay's.

"Jay would be devastated to find out his first and only child with his longtime girlfriend was fathered by his brother," Marion thought. Then Kim said Liyah's name which interrupted his thought. Marion shook because he was unsure what she said. "Marion I told you this because it's gonna come out sooner or later," Kim said with tears in her eyes.

> "Kim this all doesn't make sense," Marion said.

> "Marion listen to me. I'm telling you this because after I tell you this Liyah will probably tell Jay and

you what I'd done," Kim sighed wiping away her tears.

"What the hell does Liyah have to...," Marion said as he was cut off.

"Liyah is cheating on you! You know I wouldn't lie about shit like this," Kim exclaimed.

Marion was speechless. There wasn't anything he could say in reply. An odd shadow of denial overcame him. A part of him wanted to believe Kim was lying; however, he knew truth. He had suspicions yet he rather let her actions catch her up.

Marion put on his best facade but Kim knew he was devastated. "Hey thanks for telling me," he said bleakly. "You know I wouldn't do anything to hurt you," she said kissing him lightly on the forehead. He excused himself from the conversation and headed toward the stairs.

"Jay! You busy," he yelled from the landing. Jay leaned over the banister and said "I'll be down in a moment. Meet you in the den." Kim felt bad being the bearer of bad news. Marion walked past the kitchen as Jay jogged down the stairs.

Jay slammed the door soon as they entered the den. Marion could see he was frustrated. Jay turned on the radio and turned it up. "What the hell Jay! What's going on," Marion said.

"I just got off the line with one of my guys. He was telling me the MVB think you and Dave set up that bust earlier. He said Action said you and Dave was looking for Quintana and now they can't find him," Jay said opening his gun safe.

"Are you fucking kidding me? He trying to say we set that shit up," Marion said in disbelief towards the accusations.

"It gets a lot worse. They are bringing out all theirs hitters and shooters. They put 20K on you and Dave. I'll be damned if me and my baby get caught in this shit! I'll slaughter whoever tries to jeopardize my family," Jay said pulling out his arsenal of guns.

Marion knew that if Jay was nervous then the situation was dire. "I've called Dave but he not answering his phone," Jay said. Marion frustration towards Liyah minimized.

"Aight. Well can Liyah stay here tonight? I'm bout to run to the crib and load up then swing by Dave's," Marion said.

Chapter 3-9

It was clear that by the end of the night the drama would be at his doorstep. Jay made it clear MVB will have their shooters lurking. If they knew he killed Quintana…all hell would break loose. Action got the MVB thinking him and Dave set them up then Q gets murdered. "No negotiations taking place tonight," Marion thought.

He called Dave's phone and it went straight to voicemail again. The automated voice told him the mail box was full. Jay insisted he go get Dave and they all meet at his place. "You know I'm down! We'll all be safe if they try to come up here," Jay said checking his AR-10 and Sig Sauer Mcx.

Marion knew Jay was right. He decided "he'll go home grab his vest and artillery then head for Dave's." Jay agreed while he checked to make sure all the guns were loaded. Marion grabbed his keys and rushed out to his truck and zoomed home.

During the drive, he continuously called Liyah and Dave. Their phones kept going to voicemail. When he arrived home, he didn't see Liyah's car; "where the fuck is she at," he thought. He raced upstairs to their bedroom and grabbed his Kevlar vest, his .40 cal SW two clips and his Beretta Arx. He put the guns in his truck and left a big note on the garage door for Liyah "Meet me over Jay's when you get this!"

He hopped in his SUV and headed for Dave's. The sun was setting on the city causing the temperature to cool throughout the city. He called them again to no avail. This was unlike either of them to not return any messages. Marion began to get a bad feeling. He parked two houses down as he always done.

He walked toward Dave's house. Both of their cars sat in the driveway towards the back of the old colonial house. However, it was odd because Mya never backed into the driveway. Marion walked up the driveway towards the rear of the house.

He turned left and noticed the back door hanging by a hinge. Before he could recollect what he saw, his .40 cal SW was clutched tightly. His heart was thumping hard against his chest. He gathered his thoughts and nerves before entering. He knew that this only meant one thing, trouble.

The kitchen was in shambles. Everything cup, plate and bowl was skewed across the floor. The refrigerator was tipped over and the cupboards were bare. There was 2-3 inches of standing water throughout the kitchen.

"Dave! Mya! Are you here? Can you hear me," he yelled softly not knowing if the intruders where still in the house. He maneuvered from the kitchen to the hallway. There was various size holes in the wall. He peeked into the living room and the couches was flipped over and ripped opened. He began to think maybe it was a burglary gone wrong.

However, their 96 inch flat screen was busted and sticking half out the wall. It appeared as if someone picked it up and threw it in the wall. Everything was a mess. The tables and book cases was tipped over. Whoever did this was searching for something.

Marion nerves were a wreck. From the bottom of the steps he listened for sounds throughout the house. There was nothing but silence. He made his way back to the hallway and opened the basement door.

Chapter 4-1

Their basement was modified when they renovated. It was split into two sections the entertainment lounge and the laundry room. He descended into the finished basement. There were small spots of blood on the carpeted steps. "Something awful happened down here," Marion thought heading to the laundry room.

He opened the door and saw a big puddle of blood on the ceramic tile floor. The room was a mess. The washer and dryer had been knocked over with clothes skewed everywhere. The light of the room glistened a crossed the puddle. This was blood was fresh. Someone stepped in the blood and left tracks throughout the room.

The bloody footsteps lead to the adjacent room. Marion slowly opened the door and was overwhelmed with sorrow and grief. Dave's lifeless mutilated corpse dangled from the ceiling. He had been bound, gagged and decapitated.

His hands were so bloody and puffy; the handcuffs severed his wrist. Beneath the body was a mangled metal pipe lying on the floor in a puddle of blood. Marion saw where the killers took the pipe from the unfinished basement's foundation.

He'd been beaten senseless because his body was badly bruised and discolored from the force of the blows. There wasn't a single bone in Dave's body that probably wasn't broken," Marion thought looking at his disfigured corpse. There was a massive butcher's knife protruding from his back with deep lacerations. Marion sobbed thinking that "Half way through his ordeal, someone stabbed him repeatedly in his spine."

The killers cut his head off and bashed it until his skull ruptured. The extreme pressure made his eyes pop out and large amounts of brain matter bulge from the sockets. The once tranquil room looked like a slaughtering house. Dave's body was still warm to the touch.

"Whoever done this just left," thought Marion wiping away his tears. He knew he had to find who did this and make them suffer. He made his way back to the trampled living room. His mind raced through hundreds of unanswered questions.

"Mya," he said audibly coming up the stairs. There was no sign of her anywhere. Marion checked the guest bedroom and nothing. Walking along the hallway there was signs that there was a struggle throughout the upstairs.

Pictures once hanging on the wall now littered the hallway. His hands were drenched in sweat as he held his .40 cal. He crept down the hallway and saw their bedroom door was ajar. Through the crack door, the sun illuminated a body stretched across the bed.

When he opened the door; his heart sank. It was Mya nude lifeless body covered with blood and bruises. Marion cried from what he saw between her legs. Someone crammed a wire hanger into her vagina till it ruptured through her stomach.

There was shambles of her clothes around her ankles, wrists and neck. Marion's sorrow and grief overcame him after looking at Mya's battered face. Her face had swelled so bad that the knots had burst from the pressure.

> "Mya what happened," he pleaded under his breath repeatedly next to her body.

To his amazement she uttered softly "Please help me." He squeezed her hand and she gently squeezed back.

> "I have to get her to a hospital quickly," he thought wrapping a bloody bed sheet across her battered body.

When he hoisted her from the bed, the pressure from his hands irritated her wounds. Marion stopped in his tracks. He heard faint voices and footsteps splashing through the standing water downstairs. It sounded as if it was a couple of guys.

He quickly laid Mya back on the blood soaked bed. She groaned in agony. "They're coming back to finish her off," Marion thought. The voices got closer; Marion realized they weren't speaking English.

He glanced around the room frantically looking for a place to hide. His eyes focused on their massive closet vault. Instead of hiding in the vault, he opted to hide between the wall and the vault door. He knew from this vantage point he could take out the assailants.

> "Hacer negocios con el ca'rtel o zetas que te mueres," said a guy dressed in all black storming into the room holding a machete.

> "Date prisa y matar a esta puta!" retorted another guy walking in wearing a orange bandanna wrapped around his face.

> "Nico esperar abajo. Esto no debe tomar mucho," yelled the man in black.

"Esta' bien," yelled a voice from downstairs.

Marion listened intently as they debated with each other in Spanish. He knew he had to make his move. "Esta costumbre duele demasiado," the man in black said raising the machete. Marion breathed deeply and fired two shots from behind the reinforced steel door.

The man in black didn't get a chance to yell before his eyes widened as the hollow points dug into his body. He clutched his chest as the second slug shattered his mandible. He dropped to the ground bleeding profusely. The man with the bandanna looked at his cohort and shot at Marion. However, his bullets ricocheted off vault door.

The man with the orange bandanna yelled "vamos bebe' graza" and ran from the room. Marion maneuvered from behind the reinforce door heading for the hallway. When he past the wounded assailant, he shot him in his crown. The hollow point exploded the left side of his skull. Thick blood and brain matter splattered across the walls as his eyeball dangled from the socket.

Feeling the fear of his assailants, Marion's adrenaline was pumping. He jumped down the steps landing within paces of the man with the orange bandanna. He turned the corner towards the hallway and shot five rounds into the killer. The man with the orange bandanna grabbed his arm and dropped his gun. Marion continued his pursuit; the wounded killer slipped in the water and screamed in agony.

Marion figured he broke something by the way he wailed. However, his focus was on trying to catch the third guy. Marion noticed blood seeping through the guy's lime green shirt. At the end of the driveway was a gold colored suv. Marion shot at the guy and the suv. "Aggggh" yelled the man as he dove into the suv. The driver quickly lifted a handheld machine gun through the window then opened fire.

Immediately, Marion took cover behind the cars in the driveway. The bullets pinged, tinged and crackled against the cars. Their tires screeched as they sped off. Marion caught his breath. He knew this would be his only chance to gain information as to who murdered Dave.

He jogged back into Dave's destroyed kitchen. The injured accomplice was crawling through the murky water. Marion had so many questions but not enough time for answers. The man's breath was garbled as he choked on the water. Marion saw his shin bone protruding from his leg.

Marion squatted down beside the man and asked "who sent you?" The man replied through his excruciating pain "mal nos vemos en el infierno." Marion stared at him blankly then grabbed his head and held it beneath the water. His body jerked and shuddered as his critical organs shut down.

"You show no remorse, you receive no remorse," Marion uttered. He placed the barrel of his .40 cal against the assailant's eye. The man's mumbling stopped when Marion pulled the trigger. The bullet traveled downward and exit through his back. There was a tremendous gaping hole between the man's shoulder blades.

Chapter 4-2

The sounds of sirens could be heard in the distance. He ran upstairs to Mya; she was barely breathing. Her breaths were very quick and shallow. He whispered in her ear "help is on the way. No matter what happens, I love you." Marion ran downstairs and darted out the back door.

He peeked around the house towards the streets and saw three squad cars pulling up. "If these esseo's catch me out here, it'll be curtains for a nigga," he thought. He ran and climbed over their rear chain link fence. He scraped his forearm and knee against the brick wall behind the fence.

Just as his feet touched the ground, the chatter of the officer's radio stopped him in his tracks. He hid beside their dumpster and an overgrown thicket against the wall.

Marion held his breath as his heart thumped loudly against his chest. Through the thicket, he could see the officers peeking over the fence. The officers gazed up and down the alley before disappearing back behind the wall. "The alley is clear," said one of the officers.

The odd silence was broken as an officer yelled to dispatch "Dispatch we need medics to 4587 Oakland Lane! Dispatch we need medics to 4587 Oakland Lane!" He knew he had to get as far away from Dave's house as possible. He sprinted to the end of the alley. A police cruiser turned the corner slowly surveying the area. The officer caught eye contact with Marion and leaned his head talking into his radio.

Marion played coy hoping the officer would drive pass. The officer stopped in front of the alley staring at Marion. "It's now or never," Marion thought before fleeing up the alley.

The officer turned into the alley and mashed on the gas pedal.

The roar of the car's v8 had Marion's adrenaline sky high. He quickly jumped on a dumpster and over into someone's yard. There was a loud thud as the officer's car hit the dumpster. Marion knew Cleveland Police Dept. wouldn't pursue on foot too long. However, they would gridlock the area and run a drag net.

The sweat dripped from his forehead as he ran through someone's yard. "Stop, or I will shoot," screamed the officer. Marion glanced over his shoulder at the officer. He had unholstered his pistol and was taking aim.

The sweltering sun beamed down relentlessly. Marion approached the 6ft high solid oak privacy fence quickly. He hopped over the fence. The officer fired three times "Pow pow pow."

Marion saw splints and wood chips fly just as he cleared the top of the fence. The bullets burrowed deep into the oak wood. He ran through to the front yard where he was greeted by two small ferocious pit-bull puppies. The startled home owner watched Marion jump over the low fence and run up the street.

Once he hit 116th street, the officer ended pursuit. He could hear sirens in the distance. Marion looked up and down street looking for alternate route. The porch of a few houses was packed niggas watching the police swarm the neighborhood. He could see his truck in the distance at Chillie's Convenient Store.

However, he knew he wouldn't make it on foot. Doubt of getting away began to settle in. Someone whistled loudly and yelled "over here" from down the street. Marion didn't hesitate and ran towards the house. There were men cluttered on the porch as Marion darted in the house.

His chest was pounding and face was drenched in sweat. A dark skinned bald headed stocky guy offered him water and shelter till the police die down. To Marion's amazement there were more guys inside then on the porch. These were the niggas that keep Cleveland's crime rate high.

"Ah, are you from around here," asked the dark skinned man.

"Naah, I was just over my nigga house and some bullshit went done," Marion said through deep breaths recognizing the man's African accent.

The house was full of thugs, goons, dope boys and street niggas. However, when he entered the dwelling people began mumbling. However, he cleared the air quickly. "If any of you niggas got a problem, speak the fuck up or shut the fuck up," he said loudly finishing his third cup of water.

"Nigga! I don't know about them but you damn sure not talking to me," blurted a tall lanky brown skinned man.

"It was to any nigga in here that was mumbling that hoe shit! If it wasn't you then shut the fuck up," Marion said aggressively in front of everyone.

The lanky stood in the threshold of the living and pointed two small pistols at Marion's back. "I've never been a hoe nigga. We can handle it right here," the man retorted stepping back slightly. Everyone in the house looked on with awe and disbelief at what was transpiring. Within a blink of an eye, Marion turned around revealing his behemoth .40 cal SW.

"Whoa, whoa...y'all need to put them junts up. Nobody is killing anybody up in my shit! Y'all can save that shit for the streets," African guy said as Marion and the lanky man glared at one another.

"Maco why the fuck are you tripping! Like the nigga said, if it wasn't you then why in the hell are you saying anything," he said breaking the tension in the room.

"My nigga...I don't know what you did or why the law is chasing you; however, you won't come up in here disrespecting! The only reason you here is cuz my nigga saw you stranded out there," the African man said as Marion holstered his gun.

Everyone observed as the police raced up and down the street looking for Marion. A man leaned in the house and yelled "they're going door to door searching houses. Damn! They just ran in Screw's crib!" Everyone in the house raced to the window to see the commotion.

Marion peaked through the curtains in the living room. The police was slowly sweeping the block house by house. "Can you get me to Chillie's," Marion asked simply still looking out the curtains. He noticed police stopped and searched every vehicle entering and leaving their perimeter. "Yeah, I can get you to Chillie's," said the African.

He went in the other room and said something to some woman before reappearing. He motioned Marion to follow him to the side door in the kitchen. Outside the door was the detached garage which was in need of repair. The man lifted the rickety overhead door. Inside were a gray mid-90's Dodge Caravan and a black Ford Crown Vic.

"I need to get to my truck. I parked it at Chillie's," stated Marion.

"What the fuck did you do," said the African lighting his cigarette.

"Too much to explain. I don't even know what's going on, honestly," Marion said rubbing his chin in confusion.

"Do you have the keys to your truck? I can go get it once we get there my nigga," said the African.

"Yea…it's a black Porsche Cayenne. Its sitting behind the store on the parking lot," Marion said handing the man the keys.

"Ok. So I need you to get in the back of the van," he said unlocking the doors.

Marion opened the rear hatch. There was a huge bed and clothes scattered throughout the van. The African guy stepped beside Marion and inclined the bed. "Get in and lay down. I'll handle the rest," he said. Marion obliged. He felt the mattress recline then darkness.

His body was contorted awkwardly to fit beneath the bed. He couldn't see anything. He could hear him rustling things around atop the mattress. "Vroom," the loud van roared to life and from the vibration he sensed they were moving.

Chapter 4-3

Marion was cramped and uncomfortable. He began to lose feeling in his arm. Suddenly, the vehicle slows down to a stop. The driver said something but Marion couldn't hear because of the loud music. Marion repositioned his leg because his ankle pressed against the side railing. The volume of the music decreased to conversational level.

> "Sir may I see license, registration and proof of insurance," asked a stern voice.

> "Yea, but can you tell me why i got pulled over," asked the driver.

> "We're looking for a dangerous suspect in the neighborhood and you fit his description," said the officer.

Marion held his breath. He no longer felt the cramps in his ankle and arm. The sirens of approaching police cars made Marion finicky. At some point, the officers returned to the vehicle and asked "we need to search your vehicle?"

The driver agreed. The door chime sounded as he exited the vehicle. Immediately, the rear hatch lifted and the officers sifted through the junk. They talked amongst each other while they searched. Marion felt an officer poke his shoe which made him tense up.

> "Hey we're clear back here," stated an officer.

> "Clear up here as well," replied another.

The rear hatch slammed closed and the door chime stopped. The driver started the vehicle and drove for a while before making a stop. It sounded like the driver picked up someone; however, Marion wasn't sure so he remained silent. He began to get suspicious because they've been driving for quite some time. They were only three blocks away from the store when Marion was at the man's house.

He grabbed his gun from his holster and made one final thought "next stop I'm getting out of here." The vehicle made some turns then came to a complete stop. The music was still blaring; yet, Marion faintly heard the door chime. The rear hatch lifted slowly as the driver inclined the mattress.

Marion raised his .40 cal quickly while his eyes adjusted to the bright afternoon sun. To his amazement, three silhouettes stood before him. After his eyes adjusted, he noticed the driver had a revolver, a tall heavy set man held a sawed-off shotgun and a short guy wielding a mac-10. Marion trembled at the thought he might die today. He seen they was in a dense wooded area that he didn't immediately recognize.

The over brush was thick with debris and garbage littering the area. The area appeared to be a common dumping site. A few feet away, he saw a little dilapidated shack overgrown by the weeds. He turned his head slightly and noticed his truck adjacent to the van.

The sound of flowing water in the distance indicated he was close to Euclid Creek. "Either way, if they're going to kill me I'm not going without a fight," Marion thought.
Marion sat there in the back of the dirty van out manned and out gunned. He kept his aim directly at the driver which didn't seem too concerned.

Marion slid from the van eyes focused on the shooters. The heavy set man looked anxious. "Any second he was going to pull the trigger," Marion thought figuring his day couldn't get worse.

"Nigga you know why we're here. Don't front like you don't know what's going on! Why was the law chasing you and don't lie my nigga," said the driver folding his arms.

"What the hell you mean! I don't what you're talking about," retorted Marion stepping beside the van to give himself distance.

"What the fuck were you doing at Daveno's crib," demanded the driver.

Marion stood there stunned at what man had said. "How in the hell do he know Dave's real name? How does he know that I was Dave's house," was some of the questions he thought. Suddenly, a raspy voice from atop the secluded trail yelled "what are y'all doing down by my shack!"

Everyone looked in the direction of the raspy voice. They saw a dark skinny, old homeless man pushing a grocery cart full of junk down the trial. He shuffled along speaking gibberish to himself.

The short guy and Marion locked eyes for a brief moment. Within that stare, they thought the same thing "this is my chance!" The short guy pointed his Mac-10 at Marion. Simultaneously, Marion swung his .40 cal toward the short guy. "Tat tat tat tat tat tat! Blaow, bloaw, bloaw" was the sounds as their guns burst.

Thank you for reading

Da Streets are Callin' Me Pt.1

For more exceptional novels from the Pied Pipers of Publications.

Visit:

Excerpt:
Roulette: This is Not a Game

Chapter 1-1

Rihanna stood in the upstairs hallway at her parent's house reminiscing on better times. There were so many precious memories that brought tears to her eyes. Every bedroom felt like a time capsule. Her old room had been converted to her mother's yoga sanctuary.

She recalled being in high school and sneaking out to go a concert with her boyfriend. However, her mother caught her but vowed to never tell her father if she promised not to do that again. Then a short time after, she lost her virginity. When that spring approached, the Army called her to active duty.

Through tears of joy she laughed, because Anrico cried knowing his big sister was going off to war. He was tough to the world but sweet to the people he loved. "Ha ha," she laughed out loud remembering when her parents caught him jacking off. He was utterly speechless.

Whether, good or bad those where some of the moments she held dear. Yet, the memory she'll never forget was seeing how proud her father was to see his only daughter follow in his footsteps. He reached Double Silver Star Major General. She never saw him gleam so brightly.

However, her family drastically transformed while she was stationed in Belize. Anrico caught a murder case then her mother became severely ill. The army gave her an honorable discharge so she could attend to her family matters.

The legal system had pissed her off how they railroad her younger brother. They didn't want to consider the facts of the case. To them, it was another case of black on black gun violence. Except, her brother was properly registered to carry and conceal. She recalled the incident clearly.

> *Anrico and her parents were at Walmart when a dope fiend tried to rob her parents. They were standing at the entrance with their groceries waiting on Anrico with the car. The robber demanded their money and her father resisted then the man pistol-whipped her mother and shot her father in the leg.*
>
> *Anrico saw what had transpired and swerved up as the robber tried to flee. Through the pain, her father only concern was her mother's wellbeing. The robber opened fire when he saw Rico getting out the car. Rico's return fire dropped him quickly.*
>
> *The robber died at the scene from critical damage to his organs. Then in a whirlwind, Anrico was labeled a hero then a murderer all within a week. The police initially deemed the shooting self-defense after discovering Rico was licensed and permitted. Then an egotistical prosecutor viewed the case as a murder instead of self-defense.*
>
> *By the time she came home 6yrs later, Anrico had been sentenced to 40yrs and she had to get ready to bury her mother. They raised enough money to pay the state to allow her brother to come to their mother's funeral. Rico told her he was interested in appealing the conviction. Yet, the only thing on her mind was how "how is daddy going to handle all of this."*

However, it has been almost a year since her mother past and the house still felt different. "Anna Caine! What are you doing? Did you forget about your food," her father yelled from the bottom of the steps. Rihanna snapped out her daze and rushed downstairs. "I'm sorry dad. You know how I get when I think about Rico and mom," she said. Her father remained silent as they walked to the kitchen.

As she finished cooking dinner, the heat from the stove made sweat drip from her face. She immediately began criticizing herself for starting dinner late. It was 10:15pm and she was just now getting finished. She knew her father would be disappointed when he seen that she wasn't having dinner with him.

"He'll understand," she thought as she made her lunch. Her father stood silently in the kitchen's threshold admiring her beauty. Since her mother passed, the finances have taken a toll on his income. He hasn't been the same especially taking on her brother's appellate attorney fees.

Her father's expenses surpass $3,000 monthly. Since, she came home from the army she's been helping him strenuously. "Anna Caine, you know you're a split image of you mother. I miss her so much," her father said making his plate. She nodded in agreement.

> "You're not having dinner with me tonight," her father said surprisingly.

> "Not tonight dad, I have to work. Tonight is going to be a big night, the Miami Heat just made the playoffs. Also some of my regular clients are stopping through," she said packing her lunch in bag.

> "You know I don't approve of you taking off your clothes for money! Also those aren't clients those are perverts! King of Diamonds my ass! More like King of Demons in my opinion. If one of them bastards

gets out of line remember what I taught you," her father said sitting down at the dinner table.

"Yes dad! Also I know how to handle myself; I am a First Lieutenant remember," she said sarcastically.

She pulled back her long black hair and kissed him on the check. "Also don't worry about seeing Anrico tomorrow. Me and his attorney is going to see him tomorrow," she said before walking out the door. Every time she came to their house, she admired the accomplishments and accolades her parents obtained. Her Jeep Wrangler Overland was parked next to her father's hunter green Jaguar X-type.

Inside the garage was her mother's silver Chrysler Crossfire and her brother's custom "65" Ford Galaxy. Her phone rang as she was getting into the truck. She saw it was her stripper friend Bianca. She knew it must be something important if she called.

"Girl where you at," she said hysterically.

"I'm leaving my father's now. What's going on," Rihanna said backing out the driveway.

"The club is packed right now! Everybody is in here…niggas from the Heat, Buccaneers and some rap niggas. I think I saw the Fallout up in here as well. Get your ass here and get some of this money," she exclaimed.

"Ok girl I'll be there in 20min," Rihanna replied.

When she ended the phone call, she saw a text from one of her clients. The message read "I'm here at table 12. What time will you be here." She replied as she drove for the expressway. Rihanna hated stripping but the money she made was great.

Every day she pondered why she let Bianca convince her to strip. "Girl you got the physique, appearance and personality! You'll make enough to pay off your brother's attorney," she mouthed mimicking Bianca sassy ass. This lifestyle was for the miserable and low self-esteem in Rihanna's opinion. Nonetheless, Bianca was right about her making money.

In the few months she's been stripping, Rihanna made an average of $900 anytime she danced. She definitely made more money at King of Diamonds then at her day job. Her manager Coachella was sleazy, conniving and greedy. His short, narcissistic, burnt black, crooked smile having ass lived up to his shoddy reputation.

On the other hand, Rihanna respected Coachella managing skills. All his top dancers performed at top line clubs like King of Diamonds, Eleven and Magic City to name a few. Bianca told her that he'll either fuck'em out a nut or fuck'em out their money. Either way, Rihanna wasn't going for that bullshit.

Bianca vouched for her and got her at King of Diamonds. He wanted to put her at some third rank club. The transition from being a disciplined soldier to deceiving male entertainer never sat well with Rihanna. If anyone could make a successful conversion it'll be the daughter of Double Silver Star Major General Richard Andrews.

Chapter 1-2

The ride to King of Diamonds was quick. There wasn't much traffic on the expressway. She parked and made her way to the employee entrance. The on duty police officer White Tyson saw her orange Wrangler pull into the parking lot. He met her at her truck and helped her with her bags.

White Tyson looked like Jon B but built like the MMA fighter Conner McGregor. He was as tough as they came especially protecting the girls. One night, two guys tried to assault one of the dancers. He broke one of the guys arm and fractured the other's jaw and skull.

> "How you doing tonight Anna," he said giving her a hug
>
> "I'm doing alright Tyson. Feel a little bad for not having dinner with my dad. Yet, I need to make this extra money for my brother's attorney," she said as they walked toward the building.
>
> "I remember you telling about your brother's case. How much is his attorney fees," Tyson said putting his arm around her shoulder.
>
> "Uggh! 80 grand but we've got it down to 50. Yet, he promised he could get the conviction overturned," she said angrily
>
> "Damn! That's a mortgage. I know your brother is proud to have y'all in his corner. Anyway, have a good night. I'll see you when you get off," he said hugging her tightly.

When she opened the door, all she saw was neon lights and people everywhere. Her eyes glanced to table twelve; her client was watching Ms. Baton Rouge on stage. Every table was occupied. Bianca definitely wasn't lying; the club was packed.

Rihanna went downstairs to the dancer's locker room. Briscoe was standing in front of the door. He was a bouncer in his forties assigned to guard the locker room. "How you doing Anna? When you gone let me take you out," he said admiring her contours. "Briscoe your wife wouldn't appreciate that," she said smirking. "Soon to be ex-wife," he said laughing opening the door.

Rihanna admired the elegant and spacious locker room. Every girl had a personal booth with a mounted digital safe. There was pole section to practice, a small spa and a hot tub. King of Diamonds was beyond a typical strip club. The aroma of perfume and hair spray filled the air.

After putting her clothes in the locker, she changed from Rihanna to Anna Caine. She slipped her toned body into a turquoise top and G-string. One of the other girl's helped her with her make up. "Girl I love your body. That plump ass of yours is going to hurt their feelings tonight," a dancer told said.

Rihanna smiled but didn't reply to the statement. She swayed to the beat of the loud music getting in her zone. Tampa strolled in with a small box of tips. She stuffed the money in her booth safe laughing.

Tampa was the most seasoned dancer at King of Diamonds. She's danced for this club for almost a decade. During that tenure, she became the self-proclaim diva of KOD. It was very obvious the other girl's was terrified of Tampa.

Rihanna saw her pummel a dancer with a stiletto for using something without permission. Her reputation for violence kept the others on eggshells. It was evident she didn't like Rihanna. Yet, she didn't care what Tampa thought.

Isis and London walked and greeted Rihanna. "You came in to get some of this money," they said attracting a spiteful glare from Tampa.

"Why are y'all speaking to this silver spoon army bitch? She already thinks she's better than us," Tampa said rolling her eyes. London and Isis remained silent. Rihanna just smiled and thought "bitch! I want you to put hands on me. That'll be your one-way ticket to the ER." Tampa didn't respond to Rihanna's expression.

Tampa pulled a blunt and sack of cocaine from her safe. Isis was Tampa's personal bust down. They didn't try to hide their sexual relationship. Isis kissed and licked on her neck while she lit the blunt.

London grabbed her phone and called her boyfriend. She snorted from the sack between their conversations. Rihanna saw enough and headed out the locker room. Marquell was still sitting at his table as she made her way over to him.

> "Hey Quell. Sorry to keep you waiting," she said intimately in his ear.

> "Oh! You know I'll always wait for you. Let's go somewhere a little more private," he said licking his tongue in her ear.

She obliged grabbing him by the hand. It surprised her that no one knew of Marquell Palmer. She recognized him immediately. He was the owner of Palmer Exotics & Imports.

His high end clientele ranged from celebrities to corporate executives. Majority of the luxurious vehicles throughout Florida came from his lot. He was very polite and generous. Marquell always stopped by to see her twice a week.

The music blared as they walked down the dimly lit hallway. She saw Tampa and Isis go in a room followed by four men. One of the men asked his friend before disappearing behind the door "do you have an extra condom?" *"Damn Tampa! You fucking for the money too,"* Rihanna thought.

Marquell overheard the guy's question and said in her ear "sounds like they're going to have some fun." He held her intimately by her hips admiring her ass. She ignored his statement. Numerous red neon lights flashed "locked" on majority of the private rooms. *"Tonight is definitely a busy night. I hope it don't get crazy,"* she thought.

They found a room towards the end of the hallway. She ushered him and closed the door. The loud music was barely audible through sound reinforced room. "What's the huge bed for," he chuckled as Rihanna turned around taking off her stilettos.

That's for entertainment purposes she teased. He sat on the circular love seat eyes focused on her every move. Her light skinned toned physique swung and swayed from the pole effortlessly. She felt her nipples hardened from the continuous sensation of the pole rubbing her pussy.

Marquell eagerly blew two thousand before the end of the first song. He followed that with a $500 courteous tip. That $2,500 dollars didn't hurt his pockets at all. He still had a stack of 100's and 50's next to him on the table. There was five to ten thousand on the table. Rihanna knew one thing *"if he showed it, he's going to throw it."*

He maintained eye contact with her throughout her dance. His phone rang and he quickly ignored the call. Her body glistened beneath the illumination of the fluorescent lights. While on the mini-stage, everything was a blur as her Anna Caine persona took control.

When she climbed the pole and slide down slowly, he bit his lip in anticipation. Marquell grinned re-adjusting his pants in excitement. He threw numerous fifty dollar bills when started her choreographed floor routine. When she did the splits, he signaled her to come closer.

She stepped from the platform and seductively dog walked to Marquell. She rubbed her hands along his legs up to his abdomen. "Ooh. I like when you do that," he cooed staring her in the eyes. He ran his hands through her pinned-up hair.

> "Take them pins out your hair," he said removing her hair clips.

Her hair dropped instantly down her back. He slipped his hand along her shoulder then untied turquoise top. Her perky breast grazed his legs when her top came off. Rihanna could see his dick pulsating in his pants.

The aroma of his cologne was potent and very enticing. Tonight, she found herself heavily attracted to Marquell. His clean cut and conservative style complemented his African American/ Iranian decent. Since they met, she was his exclusive dancer.

He threw the rest of his fifty dollar bills. There was a loud thud on the door. They ignored the sound until they heard it again. "Are you expecting company," Marquell said jokingly pointing at the door.

There was a puzzled expression on Rihanna's face as she put her top back on. When she approached the door; there was a faint voice coming from the hall. As she opened the door partially, Tampa barged in the room in a tirade

> "Bitch! Where's my fucking money," she howled in Rihanna's face.

> "What the fuck are you talking about bitch? Do you see I'm with a client," she demanded getting frustrated.

"I just put my money in my safe! It was only 4 of us in there! Some bitches in the locker room told me they saw you take my money," Tampa yelled storming into the room with Isis and London in tow. They continuously instigated which aggravated Tampa's temper. Rihanna was embarrassed and pissed off simultaneously. Marquell observed quietly with a glimpse of anticipation in his eyes. He knew what was going to transpire.

> "Well since you wanna take mines; I'm gonna take yours," Tampa balked grabbing Rihanna's tip box from the mini-stage.

> "Hold up bitch! What do you think you're doing," Rihanna demanded grabbing her wrist.

"You hear me bit...," Tampa uttered before being chopped in the throat. Rihanna then yanked her forward swiftly elbowing Tampa in the face. Her knees buckled after Rihanna front kicked her in the abdomen. "Get this bitch," she ordered catching her breath.

Rihanna's combat training and military instinct was in high gear. London and Isis was hesitant after Rihanna's display of skill.

Order Form

KMG Publications
P.O. Box 53513
Indianapolis, IN, 46253

Current Titles	Price
Da Streets are Callin Me Pt. 1	$ 15.00

Pre-Release	Price
Sekrits of Loyalty	$ 15.00
Da Streets are Callin Me Pt. 2	$ 15.00
Cleveland: Badge of Corruption	$ 15.00
Tha P.O.P.E. (Pressure of Pleasing Everyone)	$ 15.00

Titles	Price	
1.	$ 15.00	
2.	$ 15.00	
3.	$ 15.00	
	Sales Tax 7%	
	Discount Code	
	Grand Total	$

Please write clearly and legible with blue or black ink. Any deviations may cause a delay in order

[ ] Credit/Debit Card

| Visa | MasterCard | Discover | American Express |

Name: _____
Card Number: _____
Expiration Date: _____
CCV: _____ (Is a **three-digit code** on the back of card)

[ ] Money Order *Please make **all money orders** payable to KMG Publications* (Address mentioned above)

Returns

You have 30 calendar days to return an item from the date you received it.

To be eligible for a return, your item must be unused and in the same condition that you received it.

Your item must be in the original packaging.

Refunds

Once we receive your item, we will inspect it and notify you that we have received your returned item. We will immediately notify you on the status of your refund after inspecting the item.

If your return is approved, we will initiate a refund to your credit card (or original method of payment).

You will receive the credit within a certain amount of days, depending on your card issuer's policies.

Shipping

You will be responsible for paying for your own shipping costs for returned items. Shipping costs are non-refundable.

Contact Us

If you have any questions on how to return your item to us, contact us.

KMG Publications, LLC
P.O. Box 53513
Indianapolis, IN 46253
Facebook.com/kmgpublicationsllc

PUBLICATIONS

Order Form

KMG Publications
P.O. Box 53513
Indianapolis, IN, 46253

Current Titles	Price
Da Streets are Callin Me Pt. 1	$ 15.00

Pre-Release	Price
Sekrits of Loyalty	$ 15.00
Da Streets are Callin Me Pt. 2	$ 15.00
Cleveland: Badge of Corruption	$ 15.00
Tha P.O.P.E. (Pressure of Pleasing Everyone)	$ 15.00

Titles	Price	
1.	$ 15.00	
2.	$ 15.00	
3.	$ 15.00	
	Sales Tax 7%	
	Discount Code	
	Grand Total	$

Please write clearly and legible with blue or black ink. Any deviations may cause a delay in order

☐ Credit/Debit Card

Visa	MasterCard	Discover	American Express

Name: _____
Card Number: _____
Expiration Date: _____
CCV: _____ (Is a **three-digit code** on the back of card)

☐ Money Order *Please make **all money orders** payable to KMG Publications* (Address mentioned above)

Returns

Mi'Shele: Da Streets are Callin Me Pt. 1

You have 30 calendar days to return an item from the date you received it.

To be eligible for a return, your item must be unused and in the same condition that you received it.

Your item must be in the original packaging.

Refunds

Once we receive your item, we will inspect it and notify you that we have received your returned item. We will immediately notify you on the status of your refund after inspecting the item.

If your return is approved, we will initiate a refund to your credit card (or original method of payment).

You will receive the credit within a certain amount of days, depending on your card issuer's policies.

Shipping

You will be responsible for paying for your own shipping costs for returned items. Shipping costs are non-refundable.

Contact Us

If you have any questions on how to return your item to us, contact us.

KMG Publications, LLC
P.O. Box 53513
Indianapolis, IN 46253
Facebook.com/kmgpublicationsllc

Order Form

KMG Publications
P.O. Box 53513
Indianapolis, IN, 46253

Current Titles	Price
Da Streets are Callin Me Pt. 1	$ 15.00

Pre-Release	Price
Sekrits of Loyalty	$ 15.00
Da Streets are Callin Me Pt. 2	$ 15.00
Cleveland: Badge of Corruption	$ 15.00
Tha P.O.P.E. (Pressure of Pleasing Everyone)	$ 15.00

Titles	Price	
1.	$ 15.00	
2.	$ 15.00	
3.	$ 15.00	
	Sales Tax 7%	
	Discount Code	
	Grand Total	$

Please write clearly and legible with blue or black ink. Any deviations may cause a delay in order

☐ Credit/Debit Card

| Visa | MasterCard | Discover | American Express |

Name: _____
Card Number: _____
Expiration Date: _____
CCV: _____ (Is a **three-digit code** on the back of card)

☐ Money Order *Please make **all money orders** payable to KMG Publications* (Address mentioned above)

Returns

You have 30 calendar days to return an item from the date you received it.

To be eligible for a return, your item must be unused and in the same condition that you received it.

Your item must be in the original packaging.

Refunds

Once we receive your item, we will inspect it and notify you that we have received your returned item. We will immediately notify you on the status of your refund after inspecting the item.

If your return is approved, we will initiate a refund to your credit card (or original method of payment).

You will receive the credit within a certain amount of days, depending on your card issuer's policies.

Shipping

You will be responsible for paying for your own shipping costs for returned items. Shipping costs are non-refundable.

Contact Us

If you have any questions on how to return your item to us, contact us.

KMG Publications, LLC
P.O. Box 53513
Indianapolis, IN 46253
Facebook.com/kmgpublicationsllc

Made in the USA
Columbia, SC
16 September 2024